Wolf Betrayed

A Talon Pack Novel

By
Carrie Ann Ryan

Author Highlights

Praise for Carrie Ann Ryan....

"Carrie Ann Ryan knows how to pull your heartstrings and make your pulse pound! Her wonderful Redwood Pack series will draw you in and keep you reading long into the night. I can't wait to see what comes next with the new generation, the Talons. Keep them coming, Carrie Ann!" –Lara Adrian, New York Times bestselling author of CRAVE THE NIGHT

"Carrie Ann Ryan never fails to draw readers in with passion, raw sensuality, and characters that pop off the page. Any book by Carrie Ann is an absolute treat." – New York Times Bestselling Author J. Kenner

"With snarky humor, sizzling love scenes, and brilliant, imaginative worldbuilding, The Dante's Circle series reads as if Carrie Ann Ryan peeked at my personal wish list!" – NYT Bestselling Author, Larissa Ione

"Carrie Ann Ryan writes sexy shifters in a world full of passionate happily-ever-afters." – *New York Times* Bestselling Author Vivian Arend

"Carrie Ann's books are sexy with characters you can't help but love from page one. They are heat and heart blended to perfection." *New York Times* Bestselling Author Jayne Rylon

Carrie Ann Ryan's books are wickedly funny and deliciously hot, with plenty of twists to keep you guessing. They'll keep you up all night!" USA Today Bestselling Author Cari Quinn

"Once again, Carrie Ann Ryan knocks the Dante's Circle series out of the park. The queen of hot, sexy, enthralling paranormal romance, Carrie Ann is an author not to miss!" *New York Times* bestselling Author Marie Harte

Dedication

To Chelle.

Acknowledgements

I feel like I write the same things here each time and I can't help it. I have such an amazing team and I know I wouldn't be able to do what I do without them. So thank you Charity for not only my cover, but my sanity. Thank you Chelle for your counsel and edits on this one! I know you didn't get to sleep much, so I thank you. Thank you Tara and KP for keeping me going as well as organized. And thank you Avery, Skye, Christi, and Kimberly for helping me flesh out the plot...and not for freaking out when I mentioned I wanted to write about a tank.

Thank you Dr. Hubby for understanding when I need to work weekends and when I started to cry randomly thinking about this book.

And as always, thank you dear readers for sticking through everything with me. I'm so freaking blessed with y'all!

Happy reading!

Wolf Betrayed

The Talon Pack continues with the daughter of a traitor, the man who can never be her lover, and another man she should never want...her enemy.

Charlotte Jamenson was born to the Pack that threatened the world, but grew up in the one that saved it. She's spent her entire life repenting for lies and faults that were never hers to bear. When she falls for her best friend, Bram Devlin, she thinks she's finally found forgiveness for the blood in her veins; only a mating bond never came.

Bram knows there's something missing within his mating with Charlotte, but there's nothing he can do about it. Their Pack is in danger, and it's his duty to protect their Alpha—even if it means sacrificing his life. When he's put in charge of protecting a new member of the Talon Pack, he realizes he and Charlotte may just have a chance at something more than heartache.

Shane Bruins sacrificed his life and his future to protect the Packs from the men he worked for. Now, thanks to circumstances beyond his control, he's not quite who he was before, and his life is on the line yet again. Only this time, he isn't alone, and the two wolves in his path might be the only things that can calm the beast inside.

The war isn't coming, it's here, and the Talon Pack will have to rely on three souls who know they aren't

what each other wants—but exactly what they need—
to win.

CHAPTER ONE

Charlotte Jamenson ducked beneath a fallen tree branch and inwardly cursed when she tripped over an aboveground root. If she'd been in her human form, she'd probably have said the word aloud and added a few others, as well. Instead, she huffed a breath, lowered her head, and moved faster through the woods.

Her wolf pushed at her, ready to take control and let the run do what it needed to: relieve the tension and stress that came with being who she was in a Pack on the brink of war. Yet she couldn't quite let her wolf come to the surface even though she was in that form. Her human half needed to think, to feel the dirt beneath her paws, and hold on to what little control she had over her life. The war was coming, perhaps it was even here, and she didn't have a clue how she could help.

She was the adoptive daughter of the former Omega of the Redwood Pack. The true daughter of the traitor to the Central Pack.

Yet she had nothing to show for her blood other than the guilt that came with continuing to breathe when so many others did not.

The other wolf with her nipped at her flank, and she sped up, thankful that he'd pulled her out of her thoughts of self-pity. She had enough trouble figuring out how to help her people without falling into a depression over where she'd come from yet again.

Charlotte didn't bother to turn and bite at the other wolf for daring to touch her. This was Bram, her best friend and everything else that she could possibly ever need, he could nip at her if he wanted. She'd just nip back.

When he tried to snap at her again, she slammed her body into his. He was so much bigger than she was, though—in either form—that he didn't budge, and she almost stumbled. He let out a soft growl, even as they continued their pace, as if admonishing her for being so careless. Either that or he worried about her too much. As this was Bram, it was probably a mixture of both.

They continued their run, their pace increasing until she was panting and losing steam. She hadn't been sleeping well, not with the steady unrest around them and the wolf at her side, and now it was starting to show. She wouldn't be much help to her Pack and family if she didn't start taking care of herself. And while this run had initially been part of that, as all wolves needed the exercise, she was going to hurt herself if she didn't slow down and head back home.

Bram seemed to sense her needs—as always—and slowed down first. She held back another sigh and matched his pace until they were both walking back toward the set of trees where they'd left their clothing.

When they reached the area, she let out a low moan, knowing the pain from the change was coming.

2

Even though she'd done this countless times before, the transition between wolf and human, human and wolf, never got any easier. For people like Bram, who seemed to excel at everything he did, it looked as if he gently flowed from one form to another. He never showed any signs of weakness, never looked like he wanted to pass out from the pain. That was probably why he was an enforcer and protector for her Uncle Kade, the Alpha of the Redwood Pack.

And why she was still caught in the in-between without a clear duty or purpose.

Her bones popped, her muscles tearing as her body completed the unnatural change between her two forms. It wasn't like in the movies the humans had made before the Unveiling. This wasn't full of sparkly magic and wishes. It was an intense agony infused with faith in the moon goddess that Charlotte wouldn't get stuck halfway between her two halves.

She'd had nightmares about that when she was little.

Of course, the fact that she'd *seen* it happen to her brother's...experiments before she'd come to the Redwood Pack probably had something to do with it.

When she was finally back in her human form, she stood on shaky legs and let out another breath. Her body was sweat-slick and achy, but the run had done her good. Her wolf had needed the escape, and Charlotte had needed to be alone with Bram. Even if just the idea of it was a sweet agony.

He was her best friend. Her everything.

The one man who the goddess had chosen to be her mate.

But when the mating bond didn't come, her heart had shattered into a thousand pieces. She'd always known she'd never be good enough for a wolf such as Bram, yet some small part of her had hoped the moon

3

goddess would allow her that one piece of happiness. But the blood in her veins spoke loudly to those who dared to listen, and because of that, Bram would never be hers.

There would be another chance for him to mate, she knew. There were potential mates around the world for every shifter in existence. One only needed to find them. They could choose whom the moon goddess put in front of them, or wait to find someone their human half could love.

Charlotte had thought Bram was hers. Her wolf *knew* it to be true.

But no bond had come.

So she would remain his best friend, and when he found another wolf to complete the bond, she would step aside and shatter, breaking every day until she took her last breath.

Strong fingers gripped her chin, and she pulled herself out from beneath her blanket of self-doubt.

"Charlotte." Bram's voice soothed her, even as it brought her to the edge and made her ache.

"What?" she breathed.

"You need to stop thinking so hard," he said softly. His eyes were dark, yet the yellow ring around the irises told her that his wolf was close to the surface. "You're hurting yourself; pushing yourself until you're bound to break."

She'd already broken.

But she didn't tell him that. He knew it already since he'd crumbled right next to her when the bond hadn't come.

"I'm fine." A breathy answer. She cleared her throat. "I'm fine," she repeated, her voice far stronger. She was good at pretending she held a strength within herself she would never actually possess. Her sister, the only mother she'd ever known since Ellie had

4

raised her from a small child, had taught her how to pretend, how to face her fears even if she may never fully overcome them.

Bram frowned, and she wanted to rub away the little line that formed between his dark brows. She loved that line, just like she loved every inch of his face, though she'd never told him that. She never would.

His skin was smooth, dark brown, and encased muscles that held the strength of a Pack leader. The squareness of his jaw, and the broadness of his shoulders had only intensified as he'd grown into himself and his position in the Pack, and she'd fallen for him early on in their friendship. Their one night of passion, however, would have to be the last time, as the bond hadn't come when it should have.

Bram was not hers, and he never would be.

But she couldn't fight for her Pack in this time of war if she spent her days mooning over a wolf she could never have.

Resolute, she rolled her shoulders and took a step back from him. The hurt that crossed his features mirrored her own, but both she and Bram were good at pretending.

Oh so good.

"Do you want to head back?" Bram asked as he fisted his hands by his sides. She did her best not to look down past his waist since neither of them had put clothes on yet. Nudity shouldn't matter to wolves, and yet it did right then. She'd once felt his body up close, caressed every hard inch of him, but now she had to push that from her mind.

"We need to," she answered as she bent to pick up her clothing. She hadn't missed Bram's gaze wander over her body, and she couldn't allow it any longer. They needed to move on, and they couldn't do that if they were constantly panting with need. "I promised Mom that I'd be back for dinner. Lana and Belle miss me."

Charlotte had chosen to call Ellie her mother when she'd come to the Redwood Pack. Though technically, Ellie was Charlotte's half-sister, it had been easier to call Ellie "Mom" and refer to Maddox as her father. They had been the ones to raise her and teach her what it meant to be a shifter in the world of secrecy and hope. Belle and Lana were technically Charlotte's nieces, but they were the sisters of her heart. As long as she didn't think too hard about the bonds and connections that wove through their heritage, she was fine. The fact that one of her best friends, Parker, was also her nephew—and cousin— because of the ways everyone had mated only made her head hurt. So she chose to ignore all of that and focus on what mattered.

Usually.

Bram grinned then, and she held back a moan at how gorgeous the man looked when he smiled. It simply wasn't fair that he was so good-looking. "Let's get dressed, then. Your sisters shouldn't be kept waiting."

Charlotte rolled her eyes and quickly pulled on her jeans. "You spoil them."

"Well, duh. You tend to spoil them, too. They're almost adults now so we need to make sure they're pampered before we push them out into the ranking of the Pack."

"Like Dad would ever let them be pushed out like baby birds in the nest."

"True," Bram said as they started back to the center of the den where most of the homes were located. The wards the witches of the Pack had put up might protect the den from the humans' prying eyes and even more dangerous intentions, but the natural landscape of the area also provided some protection. "Maddox might not be the Omega now that Drake is coming into his powers, but the guy is more intuitive than any other wolf I know."

Bram reached out as if to take her hand as he had countless times before but seemed to think better of it and quickly dropped his arm. She refused to be hurt because of the action. It was just the way things were now.

She gave him a falsely bright smile. "Yeah, you try growing up with a Dad who can *literally* feel every emotion you're feeling. There's no hiding from him."

Bram gave her a look. "Considering I was at your house more than I was at any of my foster homes, I know exactly what you mean. Getting you out of there after hours so we could sneak around like any self-respecting teenagers wasn't the easiest thing."

Charlotte laughed, the tension of the run and what would never be slipping from her shoulders. "I still think we got off easier than Finn and the rest of Uncle Kade's kids. I mean, Kade's the freaking Alpha and always knew what I was up to. Just imagine his own kids."

Bram shrugged. "Your family is so close, I'm pretty sure all the older generation knew what was going on with their entire passel of kids but let us get into some trouble anyway. I mean, it's how we learn, right?"

Charlotte smiled and continued walking toward her parents' home. The only reason she and her cousins had been able to run as wild as they had was because the Redwoods were healthy. Though she'd lost her grandparents in the final battles with the Central Pack, the rest of the den had risen up to protect their own. The battle that had taken Edward's and Pat's lives had fundamentally changed the Pack's structure and bonds. Charlotte's generation of wolves had been forced to come into their powers far earlier than they should have, and children like Bram had lost their parents in the seemingly unending battles.

From the ashes, the Redwoods had grown into a power to be reckoned with.

The Talon Pack, their allies and friends, were still learning how to become a Pack like hers. They didn't have the same history as the Redwoods, and because of that, they were technically weaker. But because they were allies, and so many within each of the Packs had mated with each other, they were almost one large Pack now—with two Alphas. She wasn't sure how things would work in the future, but for now, they had a solid alliance and shared a threat.

The humans.

When the world had found out about the existence of shifters, some humans had chosen to take them in with open arms. Others had created a war. Politics and grandstanding were now commonplace, and Charlotte's people were on the edge of a blade that would either protect them or cut them down to nothing.

She wasn't sure what all was coming for them, but she knew she would fight for her family no matter what...they just needed to give her a chance.

When she stepped into the first true home she'd ever known, she smiled at the sight of her parents making out in the middle of the living room. They'd been mated for over thirty years, and still, Maddox and Ellie couldn't keep their hands off each other. The two of them were standing close together, caught in an embrace that should have embarrassed Charlotte, but merely showed her what she would never have. At least not with Bram.

Finally, the two wolves in front of her seemed to notice their presence, and they pulled apart, but not before Ellie traced her finger over the scar on Maddox's face.

The scar Corbin—the brother Ellie and Charlotte shared—had put there in a heated rage.

Maddox kissed Ellie's palm and pulled away to face Charlotte and Bram. "How was your run?" he asked, his wolf in his eyes.

Charlotte held back a sigh and moved forward to hug her father and mother. "Good, I needed it."

Her dad kissed her temple before looking over her head at Bram. "Bram." His voice was a little rough, a little cold, and Charlotte almost rolled her eyes. Maddox loved Bram like a son, but as soon as it looked like Charlotte might be mates with Bram, Maddox had turned on the overprotective father charm and hadn't been able to turn it off again.

Bram found it funny, but it annoyed Charlotte to no end.

She met her best friend's gaze, and he shook his head. Today wasn't the day to get into it, she knew, but one day soon, she'd have to explain that she and Bram weren't what the others thought. What she had hoped.

"I'm glad you're here," Ellie said with a soft smile. Her mother always saw too much, just like Maddox did, and Charlotte was afraid they already knew the truth about her lack of bond with Bram. "Finn called earlier and asked for you."

"Oh, really?" Finn was the Heir to the Redwood Pack, the eldest son of the Alpha, and would one day be the Alpha in truth. He was also her other best friend and former roommate before he'd mated with Brynn, a former Talon Pack member.

"He's headed to the Talon den and asked you to join him and Brynn," Maddox said. "You know that we're not letting anyone go off alone outside the den, and while Finn and Brynn would normally be okay on their own as a duo, three would be even better."

Charlotte's eyes widened even as a slight thread of excitement wove its way through her. She didn't normally get picked for assignments like this. Yes, she'd fought alongside others when needed, and even helped saved some of the Talon Pack members who had been too close to an explosion, but since she didn't have a clear role in the Pack yet, those assignments were few and far between.

"Really?"

Maddox nodded. "He's leaving soon, so meet him at the main sentry gate if you're joining him. I'll phone ahead to let him know." He looked over at Bram. "Finn also said Kade was about to do an all call for the enforcers."

Bram's shoulders straightened. "At the Alpha's home, or the enforcer's place of residence?"

"At Kade's," Maddox answered.

"I'll head over there right now." Bram met Charlotte's gaze. "Be careful, okay?"

She looked into his eyes and swallowed hard. She was always careful. There wasn't another option for a wolf such as she.

"You, as well," she whispered.

Her best friend left without another word, and Charlotte was left to stare at the closed door.

"Charlotte..." her mother began.

Charlotte shook her head. "I should head out. I need to stop by my place and change my shoes. Thanks for letting me know." She quickly kissed her parents' cheeks and left without another word. She hated keeping things from them, hating hurting like she did, but she didn't know any other way to live.

By the time she made it to the gate, Brynn and Finn were already waiting. Newly mated, the two of them were wrapped around one another much like her parents had just been. Everyone in Charlotte's life seemed to be finding a mate of their own, and while she couldn't hate them for it, that little pang of jealousy still hit her every once in a while.

"You're here," Brynn said with a grin. She looked like her brothers and cousins, all strength and dark hair with wide blue eyes. Finn was one lucky wolf.

"Let's head out," Finn said quickly. "Gideon said he had something to show us, and since Brynn wanted to see her brothers, we said we'd go."

Gideon was the Alpha of the Talon Pack, while Brynn was Gideon's younger sister.

"Thanks for asking me along," Charlotte said.

Finn studied her face. "I wouldn't have anyone else."

She let that seep into her soul and sighed softly. He believed in her, and that had to count for something.

They made their way over to the Talons in Finn's vehicle, aware they were being watched. The soldiers that guarded the dens weren't on the Packs' side, but they didn't do anything to provoke an attack.

Yet.

Though Finn could have probably found a way to evade those on his tail, he let the others keep up with him. That way, the world could see that they were just simple people going to meet friends. It was all a lie, and would always be one, but she would do her part and protect what was hers. After they'd entered the Talon territory and nodded at the wolves who guarded their home, Charlotte followed Finn and Brynn to the infirmary.

"Do you know why we're here?" Charlotte asked. "I mean other than the fact that Gideon asked for us."

Brynn shook her head. "Not really. Gideon just asked us over. Kade said he'd come, but I haven't seen my family in a week so I asked if I could come instead."

Charlotte nodded. "Everything is so secret these days, I never know."

Finn shrugged. "It has to be, but I wanted you here." He met her gaze. "I don't know why, Charlotte. My wolf urged me to bring you with, and I listened to him."

Her eyes widened. "That's...a little spooky."

Finn snorted. "Tell me about it. I never used to have this connection with my wolf but after the...procedure, things are different."

The procedure that killed him, she remembered. But if Finn's wolf thought she needed to be here, she'd listen. He was the Heir for a reason, after all.

They made their way into the building, and Gideon came toward them. He had to be the biggest man Charlotte had ever seen, and that was saying something, considering how big her cousins and uncles were.

"Good, you're here."

A man's scream echoed off the walls, and Charlotte's wolf moved forward, ready to fight.

"What the hell?" Finn growled.

"That's why I wanted you here," Gideon said with a sigh. "We have a new Pack member."

Charlotte's eyes widened. While it was not uncommon to bring in new members of the Pack, they were in the middle of a war, and turning a human

12

probably wasn't the smartest thing to do. Not that she'd tell a very dominant Alpha wolf that.

"Seriously?" Finn asked.

"What happened?" Brynn said.

Gideon pinched the bridge of his nose. "He is— *was*—a soldier, working under Montag."

Charlotte hissed. Montag was the General who had killed dozens of wolves in the name of science. He tortured them to discover their secrets and was one of the loudest opponents against the wolves' right to live at all.

"I don't know what happened exactly, but we're going to find out," Gideon continued, giving Charlotte a curious glance. "He saved Ryder and Leah and risked his life to do so. Then he showed up at our borders and saw through the wards."

"Holy hell," Brynn whispered. "Ryder told me about the human that saved him, but I didn't know who it was."

"He's also the man who saved you from that bullet, FYI," Gideon said to Brynn. "But he's not human anymore."

"You changed him?" Finn asked.

Gideon shook his head. "No. That's the thing. He smells of wolf but he isn't yet. He was dying, and the only way to save him was to bring him into the Pack. He's not wolf. He's not human. He's something...different. The humans made something, Finn, something that could destroy us all if we're not careful. I don't know what to do with him."

Another scream. This one louder.

"He's in pain," Charlotte growled. She didn't know this human, didn't know if she could trust him. He was a soldier—the enemy.

Gideon nodded. "And there's nothing we can do to calm him. He's here because Walker is trying to help, but no matter what we do, nothing seems to work. I'm at my wit's end here."

Charlotte was listening, but her legs had started to move without her thinking. She moved toward the source of the screaming and sucked in a breath at the sight of the man on the bed. He was chained at his ankles and wrists, but from the gouges in his arms, she figured the restraints were for his own safety.

Perhaps.

His veins stood out prominently, and he thrashed under the blanket he wore to cover him since he didn't seem to have a stitch of anything else on. He screamed again before his eyes snapped open and met hers. His nostrils flared, and his body went rod-straight at the sight of her. Gradually, his breathing eased, and the cords on his neck softened.

Her wolf pounced, pushing at her to go closer.

But she couldn't.

Because she'd heard a word on the wind she shouldn't have. The one word that could break her.

Mate.

"Charlotte?" Finn asked. "What is it?"

She looked at him, her body swaying. "My wolf..." She pressed her lips together and pushed past him and the others so she could breathe once again.

"Charlotte," Finn said once again when he came to her side. "He's your mate, isn't he? That's why my wolf told me to bring you. Because he's here...because you needed to be. It's fate, isn't it, Charlotte? It's a twisted, fucked up fate."

"Fate? You think I believe in fate?" Charlotte took a deep breath then gave a dry laugh. "Oh, Finn. How *could* I believe in fate? What has the moon goddess ever done for me?"

Finn's eyes widened, and she wanted to let the tears fall. He'd been through his own hell with the

14

bond between wolf and man, and the bond between him and his mate. Yet she couldn't think about that, not now, not ever. "Charlotte. You can't say that. You don't believe that."

"I was born to a monster. Chained to a wall for longer than I care to remember. I watched my sister, now mother, die before somehow coming back. *I* was the one who told them how to kill my brother, Corbin, though they didn't have the chance. I saw more horrors than you could ever dream of before I even met the Redwoods. And you think the moon goddess blessed me? No. I don't think so. I might have had time with a family I don't deserve, but now what does she do? She gives me a mate that sides with the enemy. She gives me the *enemy* himself."

Finn reached out, but she took a step back.

"Don't. Don't try to make it better. The moon goddess, in all her wisdom, gave me a *human* to love, a human to cherish. That...I could do. I would embrace humanity with all my heart, even if they don't embrace us. But she didn't just give me a human. She gave me a *soldier*. She gave me a man who wants to kill us. Who wants to hold us captive and dissect us." And she didn't let her have the one wolf who should have been hers.

"You don't know that. He's not the leader, Charlotte. He could be different from the others."

She laughed, but it held no humor. "Even better. He's a pawn with no steel, no strength. He only listens to those that fear us and want to harm us." She rolled her shoulders and knew she had to be stronger than she was. "I'm done, Finn. I won't mate with him. I won't listen to the moon goddess or my wolf. He's not mine. He'll never be mine."

"I'm alone."

Alone.

Again.

She'd grown up alone. It only made sense she'd die that way, too.

CHAPTER TWO

It didn't seem fair that she should be so far away while he was stuck here, wondering if she were okay. If she were safe. But nothing was ever fair in life, and Bram Devlin had learned that years before. And though he knew deep down that Charlotte could take care of herself and would always be a strong fighter, the dominant wolf inside him needed to make sure she was cared for.

His best friend had told him time and time again that it grated on her when Bram acted overprotectively. He couldn't help it, though, especially considering the strength of his wolf...and the woman he wanted to protect.

Charlotte was his best friend, his one-time lover, and the one woman he wanted to spend the rest of his days with. That fact sent a shock of pain through his chest, and he did his best to ignore it. He'd been getting too good at ignoring a lot of things recently.

"You okay?" Gina asked him quietly. Gina was the Enforcer of the Redwood Pack, bonded to the others irrevocably and able to sense danger to the Pack from outside forces. Since their Pack was on the verge of war with the human population, he figured she must constantly have a hum along her bonds, warning her of what was to come.

She was also the daughter of the Alpha, his boss, and Charlotte's cousin. Since many of the upper levels of the Pack held members of the Jamenson family, and the older generations had all felt the need to have numerous children, Bram couldn't take two steps without bumping into one of Charlotte's family members.

Usually, he didn't mind it since they had taken him in when he'd had no one, but right then, he'd rather not see them. As a whole, they saw far too much of what he was feeling, and since he wanted their baby Charlotte in every position possible as well as by his side until the end of days, he didn't think it would be good for them to know.

Charlotte's father, uncles, and cousins were big ass wolves, who hadn't slowed down even after they'd hit a century in age. Since wolves had far greater healing abilities than humans, they lived longer lifespans. He knew of a few wolves that were over five hundred years old and had been able to hide that fact from humanity for far longer than anyone thought possible. But now that the secret was out thanks to the Unveiling that had been out of their control, the mortals were getting curious.

They knew that shifters could change form at will, though they didn't necessarily know how much pain they endured each time they altered their shape, or how shifters were made. Through the past year or so, the Alphas of the Packs around the world had slowly been letting key information about how dens worked and how wolves had human halves as well as lupine sides out into the public. Though some things would always remain secret and known only to those within the Packs, there were others that could no longer be kept close to the vest. The world had grown far beyond the ideas of hidden wolves and witches. Technology had begun to outpace the magic that had once kept shifters and witches behind the veil of illusion.

Bram wasn't sure how long the wards that protected their Pack from the humans seeing too much and stopped the violence from the outside world getting in would keep up. As it was, the government and key groups already knew precisely where the dens were located, even if they couldn't quite see them. It was only a matter of time before they found a way in, and the dens lost their security.

With each new mating of a witch into the Pack, the wards would gain strength, but they couldn't rely on a fated mate to show up out of the blue to help their den. The witches had been thrust into the public eye only recently and had their own battles. Though both the Redwood and Talon Packs had formed alliances with the Coven near them, the relationship was still tentative at best.

Things were rapidly spiraling out of control, and Bram wasn't sure what the next step would be. Though they had secret shifters within the government who had held those positions for years, they wouldn't be enough if the delegation against shifters came into power. Senator McMaster was putting forth a policy that would essentially rip all human rights away from the shifters and label them as animals that could be studied, slaughtered, or locked up in cages. General Montag had already been doing some of that on his own without government approval, and Bram figured he wasn't the only one.

Their Packs had two enemies with names, yet there were countless others that could come at them at any moment.

And yet throughout all of that, Bram couldn't keep his thoughts off Charlotte. She wasn't near him and was in another Pack's den where he couldn't protect her. And frankly, she'd been pushing him away so hard recently, he wasn't sure she'd ever let him close enough to help her again.

Just because the mating hadn't taken the first time, didn't mean they shouldn't try again.

Yet he wouldn't put her through that pain again. He couldn't see that look in her eyes if the bond didn't come...couldn't feel the look on his own face.

"Bram? You're ignoring me, and Kade is about to come back to finish the meeting."

He blinked at Gina's words and shook his head. Hell, he'd been woolgathering rather than what he should have been doing. That wasn't like him, and he didn't like that this wasn't exactly the first time he'd done it recently either.

"Sorry, I was just lost in my head." He ran a hand over his face and tried to clear his mind. He'd been called here along with the other enforcers—those wolves charged with protecting their Alpha—and yet, he couldn't seem to focus.

Gina studied Bram's face and sighed. "If you need to talk about it, I'm here. Quinn, too." Quinn was her mate and a former Talon Pack member. And when Gina rested her hand on her belly ever so slightly, Bram held back a smile. Apparently, Quinn was also the father of her unborn child. Good for them.

"I'm okay. Really." Lies, but lies he was good at telling. He'd been repeating them for years.

Gina opened her mouth to say something but closed it as her father walked in. Kade, their Alpha, frowned only a for a moment before schooling his features. As the man held special Pack bonds with each member of the den, as well as tighter ones with his enforcers, he could sense minute changes within the room. Bram hoped Kade couldn't feel what Bram felt as he didn't want anyone to have to go through that, least of all his Alpha.

"Sorry, I was detained," Kade said as he walked into the room. He took a seat in one of the high-backed chairs in the living room, his wolf's presence soothing and commanding at the same time. While Bram was a dominant wolf—much more than he let on—he was nothing compared to Kade, or even Gideon, the Alpha of the Talons. There was a dominant wolf, and then there was an *Alpha*. Bram's wolf didn't want to fight against them for hierarchy; instead, it wanted to fight alongside them and protect them, unlike how he needed to keep the submissives safe. The fact that his wolf had those dual needs was what had led him to be an enforcer rather than being in another field within the den. While he could never fully relax around Kade as he could a true submissive or maternal, he at least didn't feel the need to prove his own strength. That was a comfort in itself.

Usually, they met at the enforcer's house, which had once been owned by Kade's parents. When they had been killed during the great war, the enforcers had moved in to make it a different kind of home as Kade and his siblings had already built homes of their own. When Bram had first heard about the new enforcer's home, he wasn't sure how he felt about it. But now that he lived there full-time, he knew he wouldn't be the wolf he was today without it. The close quarters had created a sense of unity with his fellow male and female enforcers. The fact that the place held its own history gave it another purpose, and added to the feeling of home Bram hadn't had since he'd been a pup with his parents.

He pushed away the long-worn grief of losing his parents in the war and once again focused on his Alpha in front of him.

Kade hadn't aged a day since turning thirty, but Bram could see the stress he wore on his shoulders. It resembled the weight Gideon wore. The two Alphas were the leaders of their Packs and the unintentional leaders of the entire population of wolves in the US. Because the government had focused on the Redwoods and Talons at first, whatever those two Alphas did next would forever alter the way *all* shifters were able to live. Bram wasn't sure how the other Alphas were taking everything as his focus was on his own Alpha and Pack, but he knew Kade was being kept apprised. Parker, Kade's nephew, and Bram's friend, was the Voice of the Wolves, and even now visiting each Pack within the US in secrecy to ensure cooperation. Bram didn't envy that job, and he was pretty sure the Alphas weren't too happy with everything going on in their part of the US.

No wonder Kade looked like he needed a nap—not that Bram would mention that to Kade. Ever. That was what Kade's mate was for, and Melanie was good at making sure Kade didn't take on too much.

The pang of not having a mate of his own hit Bram once again, and he had to push it away. This wasn't about him. It was about his Pack as a whole. He needed to get over what he couldn't have and move on.

Only he wasn't sure he would be able to.

The moon goddess gifted wolves with mates, so in theory, he had other potentials out in the world. Yet his wolf *craved* Charlotte. Everything pointed to the fact that he should have been able to create a bond with her.

When it hadn't happened, they'd shattered. He knew she'd thought it was her fault because of her birth family, though she'd never said as much. On the other hand, he always felt it was his fault because he didn't know his wolf as well as he should.

They were both messed up beyond reason, and yet they kept circling around each other. They would break once again if they weren't careful, and Bram wasn't sure they could come back from that.

"We need to increase patrols," Gina was saying, and he cursed himself for not paying attention once again.

Kade let out a growl. "We'll need to train more sentries then because I don't want us spread too thin. Something's coming, I can feel it, and I don't think we're in any position to slack off." He rolled his neck. "I just got off the phone with Finn, and we have another problem."

Bram sat up, the hairs on the back of his neck rising. Finn was with Charlotte, and if there were a problem, he needed to know about it.

"What is it?" Bram asked, his voice a low growl.

Kade raised an eyebrow but didn't comment on the fact that Bram rarely spoke up in these meetings. He didn't speak often at all, as he didn't have much to say. But bring in Charlotte, and apparently, he couldn't shut up.

Or focus.

"The soldier that helped Ryder escape Montag showed up at the Pack's doorstep," Kade said slowly. "He saw through the wards, and was able to slide right in, even though he was in horrible pain."

Bram stiffened. That wasn't possible, or at least it hadn't been when their magic was full strength.

"Gideon isn't sure how that happened, other than the fact that the moon goddess *spoke* to him, telling him to let Shane, the soldier, into the Pack." Kade let out a breath. "She doesn't speak to just anyone anymore, and not anyone outside the original hunter's bloodline."

Bram shook his head. As far as he was aware, only Parker's blood family was a direct descendant of the original hunter, the human who had long ago killed the wrong natural wolf and was forced to share souls with his prey when the moon goddess found out.

"Shane isn't wolf, or maybe he is. We don't know." Kade's gaze looked bleak. "He's *something,* but he smells faintly of wolf, of *other*. And he wasn't bitten. Wasn't changed."

The entire room went still.

"The humans did this?" Gina asked, her hand over her belly once more as if she could protect her unborn child from what was to come.

"We think so," Kade said with a growl. "We won't be sure until Shane wakes up long enough to tell us, but that's what we're leaning toward."

"What do you mean he needs to wake up?" Bram asked. Charlotte was still over there, and it killed him that he wasn't near her.

"He's been in so much pain that he can't form coherent sentences. He was dying until Gideon brought him into the Pack. He's doing better now that he has the Pack bonds around him, but he isn't up to full strength yet. I don't know what we're going to do about him, but no matter what, if the humans have a way to change their own into...something, then we have to formulate a plan."

"If they can form their own shifters..." Gina shivered, and Bram put his arm around her in a comforting hold. They were wolves and tactile creatures. While her mate was also an enforcer, he was one of the few on patrol now, as they couldn't leave their borders vulnerable.

"We don't know what they can do, but we will figure it out," Kade said after a moment. "No one will be happy if they found a serum or whatever the hell they are trying to do. *Nothing* can make wolves but our bite or by mating and giving birth. That is how we're made. Anything else is something different, and from the way I hear Shane is reacting to it...I don't think it's a viable option. Either way, though, there will be dangers. Humans can be fearful of it or even use it, creating a new conflict. And within our own borders, some might use it to put others in danger. There is just too much in the air, and until we can figure it all out, we have to be prepared for every possibility."

He paused then met Bram's gaze. "Shane has only calmed down once fully since he's arrived."

Bram frowned, unease settling over him at the anxiety of what his Alpha might say next.

"It was when Charlotte stepped into the room with him." Kade sighed. "When a wolf goes feral or is on the brink, sometimes there is only one way to soothe the beast." He met Bram's eyes one more time, and Bram held his breath.

He couldn't breathe. Couldn't think.

There was only one real answer for why Shane would suddenly calm in the presence of Charlotte.

"You think he's her mate." Bram's words were hollow, though a thousand different emotions warred within him.

Kade winced while the others murmured around them. It wasn't a secret that most thought Bram and Charlotte were meant to be mates, but no one knew the real reason why they hadn't made it public yet.

There hadn't been a reason to make it public, as there had been no bond.

"I need to see her," Bram said suddenly, aware he was baring himself far more than he ever had before. He didn't care what the others saw, not now when his wolf scraped at him, howling for what they might be letting out of heir grasp at this very moment.

Kade's nostrils flared, but he nodded. "Go. Gideon will be expecting you."

His Alpha reached for his phone, and Bram shot out of the room before he could think better of it. He was aware the others stared at him and would be speaking of this in detail as soon as they could, but he couldn't care, not then.

He needed to find Charlotte, and his wolf needed it more. He didn't care if he didn't have a fucking bond with her, she was his mate, and damn it, they would fix what they had broken.

And this *human* would just have to get out of his way.

By the time he made it to his car and drove toward the Talon Pack, his wolf was practically in control, and his claws threatened to escape from his fingertips. He took deep breaths, using the control techniques his father had taught him long ago. The ones that he'd been forced to learn the moment his birth parents had discovered the true strength of his wolf.

That much power for such a small pup would have been too much. His mom and dad had saved Bram's life but hadn't been able to save their own during the coming battles. Once again, he pushed those thoughts from his mind.

When he reached the Talon den, the sentinels, the wolves guarding the gates, let him through, and he pulled over to the visitor's parking area. Before he could fully get out of his vehicle, he felt her.

He closed the door quickly and opened his arms as Charlotte jumped into his embrace. He hadn't been prepared for the strength of the impact, and he took a step back, steadying himself with her in his arms.

"Charlotte," he whispered reverently. He tangled his hands in her hair and inhaled her sweet and floral scent, needing her desperately. But they were on another Pack's territory, and this wasn't the time. He wasn't sure it would ever be the time.

"He...I won't do it, Bram. I don't care what my wolf says, he's not *mine*. You are."

The words should have been a balm, but instead, they scraped him raw, leaving a bloody trail behind. While it wasn't uncommon for a wolf to find two potential mates at the same time, it wasn't easy. If the wolf couldn't choose, there would have to be a mating circle set in place where the two potentials would fight each other for the right to mate with the third. That was how Kade and Melanie had mated all those years ago, though it hadn't been Melanie's fault she hadn't been able to choose. She'd been thrust into a world she didn't know, and things had escalated too quickly.

Bram would fight for Charlotte, but he didn't want to put her through that.

"I need to see him," he said suddenly, his wolf pushing at him.

Charlotte's eyes widened as she pulled away. "Why? He doesn't matter. It doesn't matter."

He cupped her face. "It does, Charlotte. And not just because of us. You know this. What was done to him means more than what you and I are dealing with."

She pressed her lips together and gave him a reluctant nod. "I left him with the others in the

27

infirmary. Walker was sedating him again, though the meds don't seem to be working well enough."

No, the only thing that had calmed Shane had been Charlotte. Or so he'd been told. Because of that, Bram needed to see this human who wasn't quite so human.

In silence, Bram followed Charlotte to the infirmary that was attached to Walker's—the Healer's—home, her hand tucked safely in his. It didn't escape his notice that they were touching more now than they had in recent times. Before their disaster at trying to mate, they had always been close and touched in casual ways whenever they could. Afterward, however, they'd kept their distance, and it killed Bram more and more with each passing day.

As soon as they entered the building, his wolf pushed at him harder than it ever had before. For some reason, he knew as soon as he walked into Shane's room everything would change. He squeezed Charlotte's hand and let it go.

"Let me see him first," he whispered. "I...I need to see."

She frowned at him but let him go. He always loved how she trusted him when he couldn't explain *why* he needed things.

He could feel her at his back even as he moved toward the open door. Gideon and Walker stood in the doorway, curious expressions on their faces, but they didn't speak to him when he passed. He knew he'd have to talk to them soon, but not then. Not yet.

When he saw the man on the bed, he sucked in a breath. Shane's brown hair was stuck to his face, slick with sweat. His firm jaw was tight with pain, widening at his temples. He didn't make a sound, but as soon as Bram walked into the room, Shane's arched back relaxed and a sense of calm softened his features.

Bram took a staggering step back at the ramifications of what had just happened.

If what Kade had said were true, and Shane had only calmed in Charlotte's presence before this...that meant she wasn't Shane's only mate.

Bram was a potential, as well.

And that meant Bram's version of hell was only just beginning.

CHAPTER THREE

S hane Bruins was in hell. His body ached as what felt like flames licked up his back and down his legs. His bones creaked as he thrashed on the bed, and he held back a moan. It was as if someone were holding each of his limbs and pulling, but his bones weren't going in the same direction. Sweat covered his body, and bile filled his throat.

He was dying. There could be no other answer.

He didn't want to die and had fought with every ounce of his being so he wouldn't, but it seemed he hadn't been strong enough. In the end, he'd only been a man in a world of power, greed, and magic.

That wasn't what he'd signed up for all those years ago.

A cool cloth was wiped across his brow, and Shane leaned into it, craving the sensation.

"Wake up," a voice urged. "You're doing so much better, but we need you to wake up."

He frowned at the man's voice. Shane would much rather sleep. With his eyes closed, the pain wasn't quite as bad. Another wave of nausea rocked him, and he knew that what he'd just thought was a lie. He didn't sleep anymore, he just tossed and turned and prayed for the agony to cease.

"Fight it," another voice urged, this one far stronger than the first. Something inside Shane pulled at him and urged him toward the deep voice. It wasn't sexual. No, it was...power. As if whoever spoke was in charge of something far greater than Shane could understand, and whatever was inside him at the moment needed to be close to that.

"Maybe we need to bring Charlotte in," the first voice said softly. "She seemed to calm him the most."

"She's at home. Where she should be," a third voice snapped. This one was just as deep as the second but didn't have the same effect on Shane as the other. Instead, all Shane wanted to do was wake up and see who the man was. Whatever demons lay within him calmed at the man's voice, and that let fear bleed through Shane faster than it had before.

A fourth voice came closer. "Keep speaking, Bram," the voice ordered. "His heart rate slowed again at your voice. I know you don't want to acknowledge it, but it's helping."

"This is more complicated than it seems, Walker," Bram grumbled back, and Shane calmed even more. He couldn't explain why that was happening, but if the pain eased even a little, he'd take it.

"They always are," Walker mumbled by Shane's side. "Now tell him to wake up, Bram. He can't stay in this state, and we need to know what he knows."

What did Shane know? He wasn't sure anymore, but since he'd come to the conclusion that staying as he was only meant more pain, he might wake up fully now.

Might.

Someone mumbled something he couldn't quite understand, and he rolled to his side, another fresh wave of pain slamming into him. He'd been trained not to react to torture, not to let the pain take control, but nothing had prepared him for this. He twisted and turned in the sheets as if he couldn't control any part of his body. He screamed until his throat became raw, and when someone helped him drink water to soothe it, he screamed again.

This wasn't the Shane he'd grown into, and he wasn't sure he'd ever be that person again.

The last thing he remembered before the fiery pain was saving a shifter named Ryder from the clutches of a man Shane had worked for. A person he had sacrificed everything for. He'd signed up to protect his people and his country, and when word of shifters came out into the public, he'd found himself on the wrong side of history.

Not all humans hated shifters. Not all soldiers were required to fight them.

He'd been one of the soldiers to protect them at first and hadn't been in the know when it came to whatever Montag had planned for his secret experiments. As soon as he'd found out, he'd tried to stop it, but it had been too late for most of the wolves in captivity, and too late for him as well it seemed.

Montag had injected something into his system, and Shane had no idea what it was.

It burned. It ached. It was killing him.

He'd gone to the only place he thought could save him. Ryder's Pack. And somehow, he'd been able to get there and find the place without dying. He'd begged for help, and they'd given it to him. He'd honestly thought he'd only have a small chance at survival as soon as he stepped foot on wolf land. He'd unknowingly been the enemy, and even still, knew his life wasn't completely in his hands.

He was at the mercy of the wolves that surrounded him now, he was sure of that. They wanted to know what he knew, but they hadn't hurt him to get the information. That was more than could be said of those under Montag's care. The wolves were trying to help Shane now, and he would accept their assistance. Even if it meant giving up part of himself in the process.

It was the least he could do after what his unit had done to their Pack and the other wolves around the country.

People shuffled around him, and Shane mentally leaned toward the voice that had calmed him, even if it had only been for a moment. This Bram could help him, and Shane didn't know why. The only other time he'd reacted like that was when he'd smelled a sweet and floral scent in the room with him earlier. Whoever had owned that scent hadn't spoken, however, so he didn't know who it was. He only knew that that person wasn't in the room with them now.

He didn't want to think about how he could suddenly discern scents so easily now.

"Wake up," Bram whispered in his ear. Shane shivered at the feeling of the other man's breath on his neck. "You need to get up. Lying in bed will only prolong the pain. We'll help you, damn it. But you need to help yourself first."

"Nice bedside manner there," the first voice said wryly.

"Shut up, Brandon," Bram growled. "Not all of us are Omegas and good with things like this."

"If we brought in Charlotte, she might be better at it," the second voice, the one that held all that power, said slowly. There was a hint of something Shane couldn't understand in the other man's voice but whatever it was seemed to raise Bram's hackles. Shane could feel it.

"You aren't our Alpha, Gideon," Bram snarled. "She doesn't need to be part of this. You saw her before."

Her. Charlotte. Could she be the bearer of the sweet and floral scent? Shane didn't know, but listening to them fight like this was giving him a headache. Though, really, he already had one so it was just making it worse.

Shane cracked one eye open and forced himself not to close it again when bright light practically blinded him.

"There you go," Walker said from his side.

Shane couldn't see the other man, or anything other than blinding light for that matter, but each of the men in the room had a distinct voice so Shane could tell them apart. And now he even knew their names. That had to count for something since everything else was out of his control.

It took him a few more minutes, but soon he was able to keep both eyes open. He started to take in all he was seeing. Two men stood at the end of his bed, and from their facial features, blue eyes, and light brown hair, he figured that they were brothers. Gideon and Brandon. His gaze tracked to the left, and he knew this Walker had to be their brother, as well. The three looked so much alike it was a bit scary.

When he finally allowed himself to look to the right, his body stiffened despite the calm he so desperately craved. This one was Bram, the one that had helped him fight through the pain with just his voice and presence alone. He couldn't afford to ask why right then as he was trying to keep conscious, and was aware that he wasn't exactly safe from those who might want to hurt him for the crimes of his former boss.

Bram had startling brown eyes, and they studied Shane's face just as he studied Bram. Bram's dark brown skin was stretched tautly over his cheekbones and firm jaw, and he'd cut his black hair so short there was only a bare glimpse of it over the crown of his head. Shane's hair had once been that short in boot camp, but he'd been allowed to let it grow far longer than regulation length when he'd been working for Montag.

He hadn't understood at the time that it was because Montag wanted his men and women to blend into the human population to be able to kidnap wolves and the people he'd wanted to change into shifters.

Shane had never been part of that, and while he was grateful he didn't have blood on his hands, he knew he wasn't completely innocent. He should have found out about Montag's true intentions long before things had gotten as far as they had. People died because Shane hadn't known the truth.

And now he would have to face this Pack and all the Packs out there with that knowledge.

"Drink this," Walker said from his side, and Shane pulled his gaze from Bram. "You're dehydrated, and since you kept moving, we couldn't keep an IV in you for long."

Shane frowned and looked down at his arms and legs. They'd shackled him to the bed with thick chains. In fact, now that he looked closer, this wasn't a normal hospital bed, but rather one that had thick metal bolts around the sides.

"You were hurting yourself," Brandon said softly, his gaze on Shane's. "The beds are for shifters when they get hurt and can't control their wolf. It keeps us safe, and keeps the patient safe."

"We can unchain you now," Walker said as he checked Shane's vitals. "As long as you control your need to bang yourself into walls and things, you'll be okay."

Shane snorted, then coughed. Walker sighed and gave him more water. The coolness soothed his parched throat, and Shane was grateful.

"Don't snort or laugh or yell," Walker said. "In fact, take a bit before you talk. You've been out of it for four days, and you've been screaming for most of it."

Shane drank more water with Walker's help as the others unchained him. Something inside pushed at him, but when Bram moved closer to unchain his wrist, that inside thing calmed ever so slightly.

Gideon, the Talon Pack Alpha studied his face. "I brought you into the Pack. Do you remember that?"

The memory of Gideon cutting his palm resurfaced and warmth slid over Shane. "You..." He cleared his throat. "You made me Pack?"

Gideon nodded. "The moon goddess, our patron and the one that created our people long ago, told me to. She doesn't normally speak to us, and the fact that she did tells me you have important information for all of us. Or maybe you're important for another reason. I don't know exactly, but we brought you into the Pack because the bonds that hold us as one were needed to keep you alive."

Bram let out a curse, and Shane did his best not to stare at the man that intrigued him so.

"How does that work?" Shane asked roughly. "And thank you." He paused. "Thank you."

Gideon shrugged, but Shane had a feeling he wasn't as nonchalant as he seemed. The man held the power of an Alpha, and Shane had been able to feel it even through his haze of pain.

"You saved my brother's life. Saved that of his mate. We're even."

Shane shook his head and tried to sit up. Walker immediately moved to help him. He didn't like lying down while the others stood around him. He was already feeling weak. He didn't want to be truly helpless.

"You risked your Pack for me, so no, we aren't even."

Something like pride filled the Alpha's eyes, and Gideon nodded. "Then earn your gift. As for the bonds, each wolf is connected to each other through bonds, though some not as strong as others. Not everyone can feel them, but the network of them added together creates a Pack. The healthier the wolves, witches, and humans in a Pack, the stronger the connection. As Alpha, I feel those bonds more than any other. It's my job to rule, to protect, to aid."

"As it's my job as Healer to use those bonds to Heal physical wounds," Walker put in.

"And I take care of the emotional ones as the Omega," Brandon added. "Or I try to." The other man grinned, but Shane saw a sadness in the man's eyes that he couldn't quite place.

"And you?" he asked of Bram, who had been quiet up until this point.

"I'm a Redwood, not a Talon," Bram answered. "I'm the Alpha's enforcer, his protector. I think they're called lieutenants here."

Gideon nodded. "Same role, different name. We have a few other roles in the Pack, but those are our immediate ones." He frowned. "Do you know what happened to you, Shane?"

Shane met the Alpha's gaze, but before he could speak, a woman walked into the room. Gideon let out a growl, but his face softened at the sight of the woman.

"What are you doing here, Brie?" the Alpha growled softly.

"I heard your voices and knew Shane was awake," Brie said with her brow raised. She looked around the very large man and waved at Shane. "Hi, I'm Brie, Gideon's mate. How are you feeling? Did they let you at least get up and try to move around before they started to interrogate you?"

Despite the situation, Shane smiled. He'd read about Brie in the past, of course, much like he had Gideon, but no one had mentioned that her mere presence could make him feel...protective and eased.

"Brie, you shouldn't be here." Gideon's words were low, but Shane could hear the softness in his voice, a gentleness that must only be for his mate. "Not in your condition."

Brie rolled her eyes. "This is the man who saved Ryder, and there are *four* of you in here to stop him if he suddenly has the idea to attack me. I know I'm safe, and you need to calm down, grumpy wolf."

"Brie, honey, Gideon is an Alpha wolf with a pregnant mate. Being calm isn't going to happen until way after the baby is born."

Shane marveled at the connections and the way they all acted with one another. They were truly just a family with their own issues and jokes. They weren't the monsters some of the humans tried to make them out to be. He'd always known there was something more than what Montag said, but seeing it firsthand told Shane he'd made the right choice.

"Congratulations," he murmured, and Brie's eyes lit up.

"Thank you. How are you feeling?"

Shane decided to go with honesty. "Like the man I once saw as a mentor turned out to be a traitor to his country and a monster. And then that same man created some kind of serum he was sure would turn me into a wolf like you and injected it into me without my consent. They didn't know what would happen to me, but before they could cut me open and see how I worked, I escaped and ended up on your doorstep. Now I'm here, part of a Pack that might resent the fact that something is wrong with me, that I wasn't changed like the rest of you are or were, and I'm just now learning to breathe again. Only I don't know why I can now, and the fact that it might have to do with the man standing beside me and not anything within myself worries me. So I don't know what I'm feeling beyond overwhelmed and freaked out." Shane took a deep breath, aware the others were staring at him like he'd lost his mind. "Am I a wolf? Did it work? Or am I going to be something else you might need to put down if I become a danger? Or worse, will I die before you get a chance to do that and hurt someone along the way? I don't know who I am anymore, but I've been asking myself that question long before Montag injected me with whatever he did."

There was a tense silence, and it was Brie who spoke first. "That is a lot for one man to feel. Wolf or not."

Shane closed his eyes, trying to ignore the fact that Bram hadn't moved a muscle during his entire speech. He didn't know why he cared so much about what Bram thought, and that worried him as much as, if not more than, whatever poison filled his veins.

"We'll discuss the serum once you're out of bed," Gideon said after a moment. "As for if you are wolf or not, we don't know. You scent of wolf, but it's different. We'll go down that road when we need to.

Any wolf who is turned needs time to learn to control the beast inside. Usually, it takes a human being near death and the bite of an Alpha or a *very* dominant wolf to start the change." A pause. "The human population doesn't know that yet."

"I'm not exactly human anymore, am I?" Shane asked wryly.

"I guess not," Gideon said with a snort.

Walker and Brandon had been quiet during the conversation, but Shane felt their studying gazes. Bram, however, was pointedly not looking at him. Why was a Redwood wolf in the Talon den anyway? There were far more questions than answers at this point, and that unnerved Shane to no end. He solved puzzles for a living, and now he seemed to be the puzzle itself.

"What do we do now?" Shane asked.

"That's up to you, isn't it?" Gideon asked.

Shane pressed his lips together, knowing the Alpha was lying...or at least partially. There was no way Gideon would let him leave the den now as he was, but there were things Shane could do to help. At least, he hoped so.

"I risked my life for one of you, but I'd have done that no matter what. I don't need to be *even* for that. I'm here because I had nowhere else to go." He paused, knowing he was changing his life once again. Forever. "You have me. My loyalty. My...whatever I am. You took me in when you didn't have to, and I will do everything I can to repay you."

Gideon nodded, a thoughtful gleam in his eyes. "You left your people—in essence, betrayed them because they were betraying humanity and the world. I get that. I admire that. But not everyone within the Pack and outside it will be happy that you're here. But I speak for my Pack and my family as I welcome you. I

40

don't know what's coming next, but I have to trust the moon goddess and the fact that you came to us when you knew I could kill you on sight. You're Pack now, Shane. Earn it. Help us save our people."

Our people.

Shane nodded, but his mind whirled. He was Pack, but was he wolf? What would happen when he tried to shift? What would happen when Bram left the room, and he couldn't control himself anymore?

Bram.

Why did Bram matter? And who owned that sweet and floral scent from before?

His life had changed irrevocably, and though he'd come to the Talons for help, he had a feeling a cut on the hand wasn't all that was required to be entered into the Pack. It wasn't that easy. Gideon was right. He'd betrayed Montag, and the General wouldn't take that lying down.

Even though Shane had spent his life protecting others, he might have made a huge mistake in coming here. His actions, in the end, might prove to be the lynchpin that destroyed them all.

CHAPTER FOUR

Charlotte's wolf once again pushed at her, and she knew she'd have to go for a run or perhaps a hunt soon. She may have just gone on one with Bram, but it hadn't been enough. Her wolf scraped its claws along her skin, an uncomfortable pinprick of sensation that had her eyes watering. The fact that she'd run with Bram, who was usually the reason she needed such a hard run in the first place was not lost on her.

Now, there seemed to be another man in the mix to push at her wolf.

Yet she had a feeling that no amount of running would help her.

How the hell had she gotten herself into this situation? She hadn't been lying when she'd laughed hollowly at Finn's words when she'd first seen Shane. When she'd first met him. How could she trust the moon goddess like so many of her Pack? It hurt to even think about.

"Are you going to tell me what's wrong, or do you want me to try and guess?"

Charlotte turned at her mother's voice and shook her head, a small smile playing on her face. Since wolves didn't age past their thirtieth birthday—and sometimes even a few years before then—Ellie and Charlotte looked more like sisters than mother and daughter. Technically, they *were* sisters, but Ellie had adopted Charlotte when she was a young child, and Charlotte had called the other woman her mother since the day she had been brought into the Redwood Pack from the bowels of the Central Pack. The two of them had long, dark hair with bright brown eyes. Though they had two different birth mothers—thanks to their father, the former Alpha of the Central Pack, finding two mates in his lifetime—they looked much closer than half-sisters with their light brown skin and shapely hips and curves.

Charlotte wasn't sure what she would have done without Ellie and Maddox in her life. They'd brought her hope in the darkness, and when her little sisters had been born, showed her that family was more than blood ties and history.

It was what you made it.

Thinking of how her life had once been, chained in a basement and hidden from the world, Charlotte wrapped her arms around her mother's waist and hugged her tightly. Ellie didn't say a word as she hugged her back, the familiar comfort of home and family sliding into Charlotte with that one touch.

"I'm going crazy," Charlotte whispered after a moment.

Ellie slid her hand over Charlotte's hair before pulling back so they faced each other on a fallen log she'd sat on outside her parent's home. The sun was shining, and the breeze that slid over them was cool, but not too cold. Sitting here, where she'd sat so many times before, she could almost forget there was a battle going on outside of their borders and that her life had been rocked from its foundation once again just by walking into the Talon infirmary.

"Why are you going crazy, my love?" Ellie asked.

"I think...I think the moon goddess hates me." Tears stung the backs of her eyes, and Charlotte cursed herself for being so weak. She couldn't be crying, not when so many others were in worse positions and situations than she was. She should be grateful, and yet she couldn't quite find the happiness she knew could be hers if she only gave in. Or maybe there wasn't any happiness at all, and her world would continue to crumble.

Ellie sucked in a breath, taking a moment before she finally spoke. "I used to think that," her mother said softly, surprising Charlotte. "About me, that is. That the moon goddess hated me. Then I found a purpose in fighting against the Centrals and found my Maddox, your father. I think that sometimes, fate and the scary world of mating and shifters takes you down a direction you never thought would be possible." Ellie met her gaze and cupped Charlotte's cheek. "I'm here if you want to discuss specifics. Or, I'm here only to listen. But know you're never alone, Charlotte. Never."

Charlotte closed her eyes and sighed. "I need to sort everything out before I can talk about it."

Ellie just smiled and shook her head. "You know, some people do this thing called conversation to sort things out."

She rolled her eyes at her mother's words. "Yeah, well, I've never been one to take a shine to convention." She leaned forward and kissed her mother's cheek. "I need to go to the Talon den." A pause. "I promised Walker I'd be there."

She didn't want anything to do with Shane, but her wolf calmed him, and the Talons needed her.

While she hated to admit it, the idea that someone needed her for something touched a part of Charlotte that she did her best to ignore. Though no one had ever treated her like an outsider because of her birth, she'd always felt like a bit of one anyway. She'd never voiced her concerns, though she had a feeling her parents, and even Bram, had figured it out long ago anyway.

She didn't have a title in the Pack, and for many wolves, that wouldn't matter. Before the humans had found out about the existence of shifters, people in her position would merely find a job within the human realm and call the den home if that fit into their plans. Now, many of those employed outside the dens found themselves jobless and stuck within the wards until her Pack, as well as the other Packs in the country, figured out the next steps. She still trained with her cousins and other wolves because not doing so was a dangerous thing for a wolf, and she would fight alongside many of her fellow wolves during any hand-to-hand combat, but beyond that, she didn't really have a role. It killed her that she had to sit on her hands and do nothing during many of the altercations. She knew it was her cousin Nick's role as the new Beta of the Redwood Pack to ensure that she was comfortable and feeling needed, but she didn't want to bother anyone. And she had always been good at hiding her feelings.

She'd had to learn early on, after all, since her father was the former Omega of the Pack, and his life dealt in feelings.

But now, the Talons needed her, and hopefully, that would lead to more responsibilities.

She said goodbye to her mother and headed to her vehicle so she could drive to the other den. Though there were underground tunnels, she wasn't a fan of them since she couldn't feel the breeze on her skin as easily. She'd been trapped in basements and other places when she was younger and didn't want to relive that feeling if she could help it.

She'd lived through one nightmare, and now, her entire life was about not wanting to live another.

As soon as she walked into the infirmary behind Walker, her wolf nudged at her, scenting that spicy, masculine scent. Her mouth watered, and she had to keep from clamping her thighs together as she walked. Her body had only betrayed her like this with one other man, and she'd learned to somewhat curb those instincts around Bram.

She'd been with other men before Bram, as she was a healthy adult female and a shifter at that. She'd liked the comfort, and had always walked away from her lovers as friends. That was how all wolves worked. Shifters couldn't form a mating bond without that sense of instinct between them, and unmated pairs couldn't have children. She'd heard that a few times in the past, a mating bond had appeared much later in pairs whose human halves loved one another with devotion and intensity, but she hadn't felt that type of connection with any of the men she'd been with.

Before Bram.

Though she'd always been best friends with Bram, it hadn't been until they were older that their wolves had begun to sense there could be more to their relationship than friendship and attraction. She'd never had sex with Bram before that first intense sense of knowing, however, because she hadn't wanted to ruin what they had. As soon as it became clear to them that they were potential mates, she'd thrown caution to the wind and slept with him.

It had been both the most intensely erotic and emotionally damaging night of her life.

Now, this new wolf, this new scent, this man she had thought the enemy, made her body vibrate in the same way it did around Bram...though with its own unique flavor.

She closed her eyes as she paused in the hallway, doing her best to gain control. She was known for her discipline, and yet right then, it took everything in her power to not run toward the owner of that scent and wrap her body around him.

They called this the mating heat, and she hated it...even as she craved it.

"Do you need to go outside?" Walker asked, his voice low enough that no one would be able to hear. Even those shifters near with their keen sense of hearing wouldn't have been able to decipher the words.

She shook her head and forced herself to open her eyes. "I can handle it."

He gave her a look of pity, and she held back a growl. She didn't want or need his pity. "You're helping him be able to control his wolf, and because of that, you are helping someone who can't help himself. Once he's healthy, he's already vowed to give us any information he can on Montag and what kind of poison is running through his veins thanks to the General. He can't help too much right now though because he's having trouble staying in control. It's like this with many wolves when they're first turned. Becoming one of us without being born into it is violent, and half of the time, leads to death. No form of modern medicine can help that. But Shane's trying to be what those humans who resent us, who fear us, are not. He already saved Ryder's life, and Brynn's, and probably others that we don't even know about yet. He's not the enemy you think he is."

Charlotte stared at Walker for a moment, trying to decide what to say. He didn't know her, and she didn't know him. Not really. Though their families had been working together for thirty years, she hadn't needed to come to the Talon den often to meet with their Healer. She wasn't sure she appreciated Walker's words, though she knew he was just trying to help.

"I guess I should go see Shane," she said after a moment. "It's not like anyone else can help him, right?"

A curious expression covered Walker's face, but he didn't say anything. She wasn't sure what that was about, but she followed him to Shane's room after he turned away from her.

She knew it had been a mistake to come there the moment she scented him.

They hadn't gone to Shane's room, after all. Instead, Walker led her two doors down to a gym where Shane was working out, lifting weights, and giving her wolf just one more reason to jump and claw. Only this time, it wasn't only her wolf swooning. Her human half just about panted for the man.

He'd taken off his shirt, leaving it on one of the benches along the back of the room, and wore sweats that hung low on his hips. So low, she could see the indentations on his back where two tiny dimples marked where his butt started—a very, *very* firm butt. When he turned, she sucked in a breath. He was cut, built, and every other word you could use to describe a muscled male who looked more like an Adonis than the man she'd seen writhing in pain on his bed just a couple of days ago. He had washboard abs and chiseled pecs that begged for her hands to grab, for her fingers to dig in. And, holy mother of the goddess, he had those deep v-lines that led right to his...

She jerked her head up to his face, heat rising to her cheeks. She was well aware any wolf with a halfway decent sense of smell would be able to detect her arousal—hell, even the humans would at this point—but Walker had the grace not to mention it.

Shane, however...he *knew.*

His nostrils flared, and his bright eyes narrowed. His throat worked as he swallowed before he slowly lowered the weight in his hand to the floor. His shoulders stretched wonderfully at that, and she let out a little breathy moan.

Charlotte cursed herself for the sound, but Walker didn't say anything, and Shane hadn't seemed to notice. No, she wasn't sure he could notice since he was currently eye fucking her the way she'd just ogled him.

This was going to be a long day.

Beside them, Walker cleared his throat. "I have another patient that came in earlier I should check on. You two should be fine here, but you both know where Shane's room is if you want to change places." He looked at Shane, getting the other man's attention, and Charlotte quickly wiped her sweaty palms on her jeans. "I know you were in here working out because you have too much energy, but you might come down off that high pretty quickly with her here. Don't hurt yourself. I'm not in the mood to Heal you." Walker winked as he said it, and any other time, Charlotte might have liked to get to know Walker more, but right then, she could only think of Shane.

Shirtless and sweaty Shane.

The Shane she wanted to lick and taste. Bite. To sink her teeth into until her wolf was finally satisfied, and the woman within her could feast, as well.

Walker left with a stern look at Shane, and Charlotte sucked in a breath, knowing it was a mistake as soon as she did it. He was just so *potent*. That sweaty and spicy scent coated her tongue and seeped into her pores. Her wolf wanted to roll around it in, and the rest of her wanted to lick it up. Her nipples pebbled against her bra, and she swallowed hard, fighting for her control once again.

"You're here," he said roughly, his voice almost a growl.

"I am." He looked tired, she thought. Now that she could breathe through the lust and think through the recriminations she'd had when she first saw him, she truly got a look at the man who had turned her world over. He hadn't asked to become what he was, that much she knew to be true. Those she trusted believed Shane's story about the injection and the fact that he'd run away. She couldn't help *but* believe, as no one would ever put their body through what he'd been through on purpose. Though, he wasn't truly a wolf...not yet, and perhaps not ever. What must it be like to travel along two worlds, one foot in each without a path to move into the one they truly wanted? Of course, Charlotte had lived that before, only on a much different scale. The fact that she and Shane seemed to have something in common, if only somewhat tangible, pulled at her wolf.

Once again, Charlotte was confused...and scared.

"You ran away last time," Shane said, and Charlotte let out a growl.

She might have run, but she didn't need this stranger pointing it out.

He held up both hands. "Sorry. I just know what the others told me. I remember your scent, though." His nostrils flared again, and his eyes darkened.

This time, Charlotte did indeed press her legs together because her clit throbbed unrepentantly.

"It was a shock seeing you." She didn't tell him why, and wasn't sure if she could. Not yet anyway.

"You tame the beast inside of me," he said softly. "I don't know what to do with that."

"Why do you call him 'the beast?'" she asked curiously. "He's your wolf."

He shook his head. "I haven't shifted yet. And whatever they added to me is different. How do I know it's a wolf and not whatever they made me?"

Her heart hurt for him, for everything he was going through, and yet she wasn't sure she could help. Yes, she calmed his wolf, his so-called beast, but what more could she do when she didn't even know herself.

"You became Pack, there is more wolf to you than you know," she said softly.

Shane's eyes flared in gratitude, but he still sighed. "Gideon tells me humans are added, and that in your Pack, there is not only a partial demon, someone that was bitten by one, but one is also the daughter of a demon. What if I'm more like them than wolf?"

Charlotte shook her head. Her family had been through literal hell thanks to the Centrals, and because of that, some of them carried wounds that had healed...differently than others.

"If you are more like my uncle and aunt, then you are well on your way to being one of the strongest people I know. Their circumstances didn't define them. It could have, but it didn't."

She ignored the telling voice within her head that spoke of her own circumstances and what they said about her. This was not about her past, but rather Shane's future.

51

"I don't know if you'll be able to shift, or if something else will have to happen, but the Talons brought you in, and they aren't going to leave you behind." She met his gaze. "Wolves don't do that."

"Thank you for that," he said after a long moment. "Do you know what you're supposed to be doing here? Just standing around so I can breathe, or do you have other things you should be doing." He ran a hand over his shoulder and Charlotte's mouth went dry.

The man had more muscles than even Bram, and she hadn't thought that possible. Between the two of them, her knees would just go completely weak, and she wasn't sure she'd be able to make it out alive.

"I don't know what we're supposed to be doing," she answered with a shrug. "They want you healthy, and it looks like I'm the only person that can help you."

He studied her face. "They haven't told you yet," he said slowly.

She froze. "What haven't they told me?" she asked, her wolf going on alert. Was there something else going on she didn't know about?

Shane took a step forward, and she instinctively took a step back. The hurt on his face was too much for her to bear, and she took a deep breath before moving toward him again. Hesitantly, she put her hand on his forearm. Her wolf bucked, and she swore she could feel *something* within him do the same. Shane froze, as did she, and they both blinked at one another. His arm was so warm, so...strong beneath her palm. All she had to do was squeeze gently and dig her fingers and nails a bit and she'd have a good hold on him. From there, she could go on her tiptoes and take his mouth.

Only she didn't want his mouth, didn't want him.

She wanted Bram, and she couldn't have him. She'd been forsaken by the moon goddess, and because of that, she had a feeling if she were to try to be with Shane, no bond would form there either. It had almost killed her once to go through that, and she couldn't do it again. Since Bram was the purest and most loyal wolf she knew, the fault had to lie with her and the blood that ran through her veins.

She didn't want this man, this human, who wasn't quite human any longer. Her wolf might feel the need for him now, but that would pass. Instead of succumbing to her hormones, she'd back away and do her duty before locking herself away once more. It was the only way she could stay sane.

It had been working for the past few years, and damn it, it would just have to keep working.

"What haven't they told me?" she asked again.

Shane was the one to pull away this time, and though she immediately felt the loss, she was grateful.

"You're not the only one who can calm the beast inside me."

How could that be possible? She wasn't sure that Shane knew about mating and how everything that came with that worked, and because of that fact, she didn't mention it just then. She didn't have the words or the energy to venture down that path. But if someone else could calm him, maybe it wasn't mating heat and wolf actions that were at play here. Maybe it was something else.

Or maybe...maybe Shane had a second potential mate within his reach.

"Who..." She cleared her throat. "Who else?"

"Me."

She whirled at the sound of Bram's voice, her claws sliding from her fingertips, and her wolf slamming forward. She'd been so caught up in Shane,

53

she hadn't known Bram was so close. Her wolf clawed at her, and her body shook, even as she forced her claws to retract. Bram could calm Shane? How was that possible?

Bram met her gaze but didn't say anything. There were so many words left unsaid between them, so many promises that would never be kept if they continued on as they were.

"Bram." Her voice was a whisper, yet in the quiet gym with only the sound of their breathing and heartbeats to take up the space, it sounded like a scream.

"I didn't quite believe it myself," Bram said after a moment. He looked over Charlotte's shoulder then. "It's good to see you out of bed." He raked his gaze along Shane much as she had before, and Charlotte had a sinking feeling things weren't as they seemed.

"It's good to be out of bed," Shane answered. "I take it you two know each other."

Charlotte turned so she faced the two of them. They made a triangle, three points, three connections, three souls who she feared would never be the same after this moment.

"We do," she said, her voice annoyingly shaky.

"We're both Redwoods," Bram said after a moment. "That much you already knew. The two of us have been friends since we were children."

Shane frowned between them, seeming to sense the unspoken history and tension. "And yet you didn't mention to her that you've come to see me a couple of times to help me heal?"

Charlotte turned to Bram, glaring. "You have?"

Bram shrugged, but she could see the anger in his eyes. "You didn't seem like you were coming back, and he needed help."

"You could have told me," Charlotte snapped. "You know what this means, and yet—" She cut herself off, aware Shane was watching them with avid interest. "You know what, I'm going to go. I need to think about what all of this means, and I can't do that here."

She stormed away but stopped at the door, looking over her shoulder as she spoke, "I'm glad you're out of bed, Shane. I'm sorry... I'm just sorry."

She left Bram and Shane to speak to each other in the gym, unsure what to think. One part of her hoped Bram would explain everything so she wouldn't have to, but, of course, that made a coward out of her.

She just hadn't been prepared for the magnitude of what she'd just seen and felt. She'd figured Shane was her potential mate and knew Bram was as well despite the fact that they couldn't bond.

But if Bram and Shane were *also* potential mates... Did that mean the *three* of them were a different kind of potential when all together? She'd known of some triads, but only knew one personally. Her aunt and uncles were a rare triad in that they held the trinity bond, a bond that had its own sense of magic and wonder and strength.

Charlotte wasn't sure there could be two trinity bonds in existence, and while people lived in triads, she didn't know if those were bonded matings. She'd never asked, and now she felt all the fool for not doing so.

Could Shane and Bram not only be her mates but be mates with each other? If that were the case, could they become a true triad? Even if that were true, she was still broken. Her birth father's sins had marked her as someone who couldn't find the happiness she craved, of that much she was sure.

But what if she and Bram had needed Shane to complete their bond?

She pushed that thought from her head as soon as it showed up. She couldn't focus on that, not when the rest of her reeled, and there were far greater threats going on in the outside world. She couldn't be selfish and spend all her time worrying about her mating.

And yet...something had shifted once more.

Once she was able to breathe again, she would find the two men who had altered her reality and figure out what to do. But for now, she did the only thing she could think of when her mind was too full.

She ran.

CHAPTER FIVE

"**Y**ou aren't going to tell me, are you?" A growl.

"I can't. Not yet. She's not ready." A clench of fists.

"And me? Don't I have a right to know why you two do what you do to me? And why she's so scared of whatever it is?"

"I'll tell you. I promise. But I need to make sure she's okay."

A pause. "Good. Because I think she needs more than she's saying."

Bram shook his head, pushing out the conversation he'd had with Shane the day before. Or at least, trying to. The idea that Shane could know so much about what Charlotte needed, even if he couldn't quite articulate it, should have grated on Bram, but instead, it just pushed him further toward a conclusion he wasn't sure anyone was ready for.

His wolf wanted Charlotte *and* Shane. While others would find themselves in a position where they would have to make a decision about *which* to choose, Bram wasn't sure that was the case for them. They each had a push, a connection to the other two, and that meant there was more going on than a simple case of two potential mates in one place. There would be no mating circle this time.

They could be a true triad.

Claws dug gently at his side, and he cursed, rolling to the ground to get out of the way of another swipe. He quickly got to his feet and growled.

Quinn, his fellow enforcer, shook his head. "Get your mind in the game, man. You're lucky I was pulling my punches just then, or I could have seriously hurt you. You don't want me to have to pull in the Healer during training, do you?"

Bram shook his head and sighed. "Sorry. I won't let that happen again."

Quinn studied him, the two of them paused during their fight while the others continued their practice around them. They were on Redwood Pack land now, half of the enforcers from Bram's Pack and half of the lieutenants from the Talon Pack had come to train together. They alternated who trained and which den they were at not only to keep them on their toes but also to make sure they kept up the border patrols and ensured that their Alphas were safe. They hadn't always fought together like this, as one, sharing so many secrets; however, when they had formed an alliance thirty years ago, they had slowly started trusting each other more and more. It had taken Quinn and Gina mating over fifteen years ago for the two Packs to truly fall into their treaty, and with each subsequent mating across boundaries, their Packs were becoming woven together as one larger unit.

Though their bonds would always be with their respective Alphas, some Redwoods lived on Talon land and vice versa if their talents were able to help out the other den more than their own. That had never been an option for Bram as he had always known with the strength of his wolf that he'd be an Alpha's enforcer, but he liked the idea that their world was just that much bigger at a time of so much unrest.

"You're in your head again," Quinn snapped, pulling Bram from his thoughts. "What the hell is going on with you?"

Bram just gave Quinn a look. As a former Talon Pack member, Quinn was up to date on just who was currently in the Talon infirmary. While it wasn't a secret between the two Packs, Quinn had grown up with the Brentwoods, and therefore knew things before a lot of the Redwood population.

Quinn sighed. "How am I supposed to know if that's what you're really thinking? I mean, seriously, Bram, you're so closed off sometimes, I never know what's going on in that head of yours."

"While I usually don't shut up," Max Brentwood, the Talon Alpha's cousin and new lieutenant said with a smile. The wolf was always smiling it seemed, even in times of danger. Bram didn't understand it.

Quinn smiled widely when Max strolled up to him. Like Bram and Quinn, Max was shirtless, sweaty, and had a few nicks and cuts from claws. They fought with claws out, but only when they weren't punching as hard as they could in a true attack. When they were trying to increase their form, they kept claws in and fought that way, as well. While they could use weapons and any number of things thanks to technology, they were stronger and faster using their own gifts. So they learned how to shoot, and how to use military strategy, but they would always be wolves and Pack first.

"You don't shut up," Quinn agreed. "I'm not sure how your family can stand you since most of them are so growly they make a bear with a thorn in its paw look happy."

At that, Bram cracked a smile. It was true that many of the Brentwoods weren't the...cheeriest of wolves, but he couldn't blame them considering what they'd lived through before they'd eventually taken over the Pack from the older generation that had threatened everyone's lives.

"They can't help but love me," Max said with another grin. "And I know I was eavesdropping, but we're all wolves here, so it's not like we can help but listen." He winked, and Bram had to roll his eyes. If Bram didn't know any better, he would have thought Max was the Omega of the Talon Pack, not Brandon. You just couldn't quite stay angry or upset around the other wolf.

"It's fine," Bram bit out, though not angrily. While the other wolves had been listening, he and Quinn hadn't been using specifics. While some might know parts of the story, he didn't want anyone to know the full extent of it except for the three people who mattered. Thankfully, those who knew more than others were giving the three of them space. For now, at least.

"You're not, but I get it," Max put in. "And I know you're going to hate what I say next, but you might have to actually do something you hate in order to fix the situation."

"And what is that?"

"Talk to them." Max shrugged, and Quinn let out a snort.

Bram glared at the two of them. "I talk." Just not as much as others. Namely Max.

"When you need to, yeah," Quinn put in. "But we're not talking about the fact that you have this broody and silent vibe going on. I know you don't like speaking about what's going on in that head of yours, but you're going to need to if you are going to figure this out. Believe me, man, I messed up before and almost lost it all when I didn't say what I needed to say."

They were oh so careful not to actually mention what was going on, and Bram was grateful for that, but he didn't need to talk to these two about what was going on in his head. That would be for Charlotte, and even Shane, once he got to know the other guy more.

"Let's get back to training," Bram said finally.

The others shared a look but nodded. "Two on one?" Quinn asked.

That seemed to be the theme of his life recently. Bram raised a brow and grinned. "Deal."

Max and Quinn each pounced then, their claws tucked in, meaning they were going to fight with full force. Game on.

Bram ducked and kicked, his fist shooting out and connecting to Max's jaw even as he rolled out of the way of Quinn's punch. While the other two were very, *very* strong wolves, Bram was that much stronger. He still couldn't win this fight without either cheating a bit or getting help from another. In a real fight, he'd cheat like hell because it was life or death, but right then, he just needed to hone his skills. Max was one fast wolf, but Bram knew one wolf who was even faster.

And he could scent her coming his way.

The other enforcers and lieutenants had already dispersed, their training over for the day. While a couple lingered to watch the fight, the others left, having already seen it before. Bram enjoyed grappling with these two and did it as often as he could. They each had different strengths, and training with them helped Bram immensely.

But that scent was coming closer, and he and his wolf wanted nothing more to do with Max and Quinn. They wanted Charlotte and everything she brought with her.

With one last kick to Quinn's thigh, Bram held up his hands and called it a day. Max gave Bram a knowing grin and headed off with Quinn to get some water. Bram had needed that bout, but his wolf was still on edge, far too close to the surface to be near Charlotte.

When she came up to him, a tentative smile on her face, he was lost. She'd always had shadows in her eyes, even before he'd truly gotten to know her when they were children, and then later young adults who had become best friends. He supposed that anyone who went through what she had gone through would end up a little scarred and full of shadows. Her family had done so much to heal that, but he wasn't sure anyone would be able to fully escape the past that haunted her. And even if she could, he was pretty sure she was the one who would have to do it, not those who loved her.

When he and Charlotte had found out they were potential mates and then found out the bond hadn't worked, he'd put even more shadows in her eyes. He hated himself for that, but now he had a small inkling of hope, something he didn't normally have. If Shane were *theirs*, that meant there was a chance the bond would take this time. Maybe some of the darkness that wrapped itself around her would fade away.

Maybe this human that wasn't so human anymore would be the light to their dark.

But they couldn't do anything until they talked it out, and he wasn't sure any of them were ready for that.

Charlotte came to his side, a water bottle in one hand and a towel in the other. She had a cross-body bag strapped over her, and she'd pulled her hair back into a loose braid that hung over one shoulder.

"You guys looked like you were having fun out there," she said as she handed him the water.

He took it from her and their fingers brushed, sending shivers over his skin and a slight gasp escaping from her mouth. He drank the water down quickly, needing something for his mouth to do other than ravage her right then. His wolf pushed at him, and he barely held it together. If he weren't careful, he'd push aside the idea that they needed to talk or that they needed time, and his wolf would take over. He'd end up taking her right then and there on the grass for anyone to see, marking her as his and rutting like a damn animal.

He had more control than that. Barely, it seemed.

When Charlotte moved forward and kissed his cheek, he sucked in a breath. His wolf clawed at him, beyond tired of waiting for what was theirs. The mating heat had turned into a frenzy long ago, and now he wasn't sure he could handle her being so close to him. He took a step back and called himself all kinds of fool for putting that hurt look on her face.

He cleared his throat. "I'm sweaty," he tried to explain. Not a lie, but not the truth either.

She pressed her lips together and calmly handed him the towel. He was surprised she didn't throw it at him as he deserved.

"I'm headed to the Talons to see Shane." At the sound of the other man's name on her lips, his wolf bucked him again, wanting them both. Any other situation would have lead to jealousy, but as always, Bram and Charlotte—now Shane, as well—were a special case.

She rolled her shoulders and tugged at her braid, clearly nervous at his reaction. Since he hadn't said anything, she continued. "He says he really wants to help with what he knows, but he's having trouble keeping it together long enough to do anything. He seemed...better the last time I saw him, but that could have just been because I was there." She sighed. "I just don't know."

Bram ran the towel over his face and drank the last of the water. "Let me go take a shower and I'll go with you."

She rolled her eyes. He sort of loved it when she did that. "I can do this on my own, you know. I'm a big girl."

"I'm going with you," he growled, his wolf once again pushing him. Maybe if he took a quick cold shower and took himself in hand, he'd keep his wolf at bay for just a bit longer. He couldn't keep going like this.

"Fine," she said after a moment.

"Come with me."

Her brows rose. "You want me to take a shower with you?"

He held back a groan and the image of her in the shower with him, all slick and wet and *his*. "I meant come with me to the house...but next time..." He paused. His voice was low, a mere growl when he spoke next. "Next time, I want you with me."

Her eyes darkened, and she licked her lips. He imagined that mouth wrapped around his cock. "But we should talk about what all of this means first." Her voice was a raspy breath, and he licked his own lips.

"We will." He cleared his throat. "You're in a hurry, so let's get moving."

The abrupt change in his tone caught both of them off guard. "Lead the way," she said, her voice cool.

He took the quickest shower of his life, and because he knew she was *right* outside his bathroom door, sitting on his bed while he was in there, he didn't rub one off. So now he was clean but rock-hard. From the scent coming off her, though, he knew he wasn't alone in his need. One day, he prayed they wouldn't be in a constant state of arousal. It was killing him day by day.

They spoke only of Pack matters in the car, both careful to keep their distance. He hated what had become of them, but maybe things would change soon. He could only hope, even if something like this had never been on his radar. When they reached the Talon den, Max greeted them.

"I heard you were coming," Max said. "I figured I'd walk with you to the infirmary before I go meet with Gideon."

Bram narrowed his eyes. "We need armed guards now?"

Max rolled his eyes and leaned forward to kiss Charlotte on the cheek in hello. Bram let out a low growl. Instead of looking worried, though, the other man just shrugged before pulling away.

"No need for guards. I just thought I'd come say hello."

"Well, thank you," Charlotte said with a snort. However, Bram noticed she didn't lean toward Max. In fact, she did her best to not go near him at all. Apparently, Bram hadn't been able to hide from her how close to the surface his wolf truly was. She was acting like someone who knew what she was doing around very dominant wolves in a temper.

It shouldn't surprise him, and yet he was slightly ashamed he didn't have better control.

They walked in easy silence as they made their way to the infirmary. The Talon den was much like the Redwoods' since the two dens were situated within the same National Park, just on different ends of it. They used the natural landscape as not only protection but also as guidelines for where they built homes and other buildings.

Max began asking Charlotte a bit about council matters since Max was not only a lieutenant but also on the ruling Redwood and Talon council that had been put together a couple of decades ago. Charlotte wasn't a member, but much of her family was, and he was pretty sure she was in consideration for taking over one of the former Redwood's roles. As the original council had been made up of people who were now mated within the Packs, it constantly shifted around to make sure the needs of the Packs were met.

When they reached the infirmary, Max said goodbye before trotting off. The man was always in constant motion, and Bram could never understand it.

"I wonder why Shane is still here," Charlotte said softly.

Bram frowned at her. "What do you mean? He's a Talon now. Of course, he's in the Talon den."

She shook her head. "No, in the infirmary. He's physically healthy, if a little bruised. He shouldn't need the Healer as long as he keeps on the path he has been. And you and I are here to help him. I just don't understand."

Now that she mentioned it, he was a little confused, as well. The Healer's home was usually attached to the clinic or infirmary, and generally only housed wolves who truly needed medical care. Shane didn't exactly fall into that category, and if they were trying to make him feel welcome, cutting him off from the others didn't seem the way to do it.

"We'll ask Walker when we get in there," he said after a moment.

"Ask Walker what?" the Talon Healer asked as Charlotte and Bram passed his office. With so many wolves around, it was truly hard to pick out scents if you weren't trying, and Walker had even gone so far as to pad his office so it was hard to hear conversations. That made sense, as privacy was vital in Walker's line of work.

Bram inhaled then, now aware that there was one more scent in Walker's office.

Shane.

The other man was dressed in jeans and a long-sleeved shirt along with work boots and a belt, but he didn't look happy to be out of sweats or scrubs.

"We were just wondering why Shane is here rather than somewhere else," Charlotte answered. She looked around Walker's large body and gave Shane a smile. "Hi, sorry to talk like you're not here. The question popped into my mind when we walked inside."

Shane had been sitting when they'd arrived, but at her voice, he stood, his body long, built, and hard. Bram pushed at his wolf once more. With Charlotte and Shane near, he was going to test his control more now than any time before.

"Walker will have to answer that," Shane said, his voice low.

Bram met Walker's gaze, and the other man gave him a pained expression. "Is there a reason he's being confined here? You asked Charlotte and me to come here to help him, and you want what he can give you, but what are you giving him? He's Pack, Walker."

Shane let out a small growl, seeming to surprise himself. Bram couldn't blame the man. He had enough issues with his wolf, and he'd been born one, not changed like Shane. And the fact that Shane wasn't *truly* changed just made it that much harder for the other man. They didn't know what Shane exactly was, and with each passing day, they seemed to have more questions than answers.

That's when the light dawned for Bram.

"You're keeping him here because people are afraid of what his existence means," Bram bit out.

This time, it was Charlotte who growled.

Walker sighed and ran his hand over his face. He waved at them to come into his office fully. Now, the four of them stood around Walker's desk—Charlotte angry as hell, Shane resigned, and Bram on the edge of a fury he couldn't quantify.

"It's not safe right now," Walker began. "There are threats against him." He sighed. "Brandon and Kameron can feel them along their bonds."

Charlotte let out a curse. "Brandon is the Omega so he's sensing others are *feeling* dangerous things. But Kameron? He's the damn Enforcer. He senses attacks from *outside* forces."

"And they're both sensing something is coming, and it has to do with Shane," Walker bit out.

"Then what can I do about it?" Shane asked, clearly annoyed with being talked about as if he weren't in the room. "I'm not going to hurt your people. I refused to do it before, and I'm not going to now."

"They're your people, too," Bram put in. "That's what I'm not getting, or rather, what I didn't get until right now. They aren't worried you're going to come out and attack them. They're worried about what you represent. They don't want any evidence of the serum out there at all."

Walker pinched the bridge of his nose. "Got it in one."

"I'll help you destroy the serum," Shane said after a moment. There wasn't anger in his tone, and that pissed Bram off. The other man was giving in because he cared about others, not about himself. Why couldn't people see that? "I already said that."

"But it's still in your veins," Walker sighed. "And that's why there are threats."

Charlotte growled. "Then fucking do something about it."

Bram knew he was going to cross a line with what he was about to say, but this man, this Shane could be his *mate*, and he was damned if he'd see others hurt him.

"Then let us bring him into the Redwood Pack. Finn will blood bond him in, and we'll protect him if you can't. We already have demons in our Pack. We can handle anything."

Charlotte gave him a wide-eyed looked that matched Shane's.

This time, it was Walker who growled. "We can fucking protect him, damn it. It's much more complicated than that." He looked over at Shane, who gave him a nod. Apparently, the other man already knew this next part. "He hasn't shifted yet, so we don't know what that will do to him or the Pack bonds." Walker met Charlotte's eyes, then Bram's. "And Gideon thinks Shane *can't* leave the Talon Pack and join the Redwoods." A meaningful pause. "Ever."

Charlotte sucked in a gasp, and Bram reached out instinctively to grip her shoulder. It was the only thing he could do then when his own world had been rocked. Beyond the idea that the blood in Shane's veins could hold the chemicals that humans could use to make wolves, there was something much more going on. When wolves mated outside their Pack, they had to choose which Pack to join, some leaving behind their old Pack. For most, it was an easier decision because one wolf would have a stronger place within their respective Pack.

If Shane couldn't leave the Talons and the three of them ended up mating, Bram and Charlotte would have to leave the Redwood Pack. The Pack he had grown up in. The Pack that had taken Charlotte in when she'd had no one. He would no longer be the Alpha's enforcer, and Charlotte would no longer have the close bonds with her family.

It seemed the moon goddess and fate had once more thrown a wrench into their plans...if they had any additional plans at all.

Walker slid a hand over his head. "I'll try to get him a place to stay." He looked over at Shane. "You shouldn't have to be stuck with me day in and day out."

Shane frowned. "I'd like a...home. I haven't had one since I was a teenager." He shrugged. "Barracks don't really count, you know?" He looked over at Bram and Charlotte. "Are you two ever going to tell me why you calm me? Or why you're helping me so much? Or is this just going to be another secret?" He paused. "Why do I feel this...connection between the three of us? Is it just my wolf?" He gave a hollow laugh. "So many questions, and yet I don't think I'm going to get any answers today."

Bram shook his head. "Heal first. Answers later."

Shane let out a growl but didn't say anything. Bram wasn't sure he had the answers anyway. Things were getting more and more complicated, and that was just things with the three of them. Soon, they'd have to deal with the rest of the world.

And Bram was afraid that was where things would truly go to hell.

PARKER

Parker inhaled the crisp mountain air that had been part of him for so long. He was home. Finally. He'd been away from the Redwoods for years, at first laying the groundwork for peace within the multiple Packs around the country, then forced to put the plans into action once the Unveiling hit.

He hadn't been fully successful, but he knew there was a chance the wolves could come together as one against the humans if that ever came to fruition. The problem with how things were now, however, was that though the Redwoods and Talons were on the same page, none of the other Packs were. They were either in hiding or wanting to go about things differently.

It was Parker's job to find middle ground. It wasn't easy, and he was freaking exhausted. But now he was home for a little while, and he could see his family. He'd missed new matings, birthdays, and devastating loss.

He was home.

He just hoped he could do some good with the time he'd spent outside the den walls.

Exhaustion crept into his bones, and he really needed a nap—a nap that lasted forty hours. He'd met with every single Alpha in the US and in Europe. He hadn't been able to meet with any of the others, as they were even more shrouded in secrecy than the wolves here. He didn't know if he'd done any good, but no matter what, he knew *something* would have to happen soon. The tension within each Pack was at an all-time high, and he could even feel it within the bonds to his own Pack.

He sighed then. It had been so long since he'd truly felt the bonds to his own. They'd always been there, sure, but coming home made them flair once more, pulsating between him and his Alpha, his family, and those with special connections to the moon goddess.

As a child, he hadn't had that, and he hadn't known what he'd been missing. His Uncle Logan and mother had escaped the Talon Pack back in the days of the old Alpha's reign because of Parker's birth. He was the birth son of a traitor, adopted son of a Redwood, with the heart and soul of a true leader. Without his father, North, he wasn't sure he'd have become the man he was today.

"Parker!"

He turned at the sound of Charlotte's shout, a grin forming on his face even through his exhaustion. Charlotte was his favorite cousin, though he was sure never to tell the others that. They were similar in age, and had come to the Pack later on in life, adopted in when their childhoods were torn apart. Their adoptive fathers were brothers, twins in fact, and that had always made them close.

He'd been gone so long, though, that he'd missed what had put the new shadows in her eyes. He would have thought by now she'd be mated to Bram, perhaps thinking of having a child of her own, but that wasn't the case. Instead of asking, he pushed those thoughts away and opened his arms for her.

She threw herself into his hold and tightened her grip. "I didn't know you were coming home! You didn't say anything the last time we talked."

He kissed her temple and hugged her close, needing her wolf more than he thought possible. She was family, home. He hadn't known how much he needed her and the rest of them to center him.

He was getting older, his wolf a little wilder. What he truly needed was a mate and to start the next journey of his life. But with the government sanctions for wolves on the horizon, and this other player, General Montag, in the wind, he was afraid his time wouldn't be coming for far too long.

And Parker wasn't sure his wolf had that time to give.

When he pulled away and cupped her face, he frowned. "What happened, Charlotte?"

She looked at him, and his brave and strong Charlotte, the same girl who hadn't cried when her world had fallen apart and she'd had to pick herself up out of the ashes, burst into tears.

"Oh, baby," he soothed as he held her close once more. "Tell me everything."

"It's all wrong, Park. Everything." Her words were sobs, and he knew it was killing her to break down like this.

"Tell me."

And when she did, he knew there was a reason he'd come back. His family needed him. The world had changed once before, and here it was, shifting on its axis again. His wolf might desperately need a mate, but before he could worry about himself, he needed to ensure that his family was safe.

That was what he'd been raised to do, and damn it, he was a Redwood.

Family first. Pack first. His wolf would just have to wait.

He only prayed he had enough time.

CHAPTER SIX

S hane stood in his new home, his body tense and his mind going in a thousand different directions. He couldn't quite understand how he'd ended up in the middle of a wolf den with a new life and the loyalties he'd once held so close torn away forever.

He'd grown up with two parents who'd tried to love him but worked themselves to death trying to raise him and keep a roof over their heads. His mother had died when he was a teenager, his father the month after Shane graduated high school. He'd had no family, no close connections, nothing holding him to the ramshackle house he'd lived in, and had eagerly joined the military to find some sense of belonging.

And he'd found it, that was for sure. He'd worked his ass off, learned to be the man he was today, fought for his country, and had made a new family out of the men and women he fought side-by-side with.

He hadn't always agreed with every decision those in higher positions made, but it hadn't been his job to go against them. He'd done his duty, and he'd been proud. It wasn't until the Unveiling that things had gone awry.

He'd come to the Talon den that fateful day with the rest of his division, but he hadn't fired a round. He'd been there on orders from his commanding officer to oversee the world finding out about the existence of shifters from this tiny part of the US. And in the year between the Unveiling and the rise of General Montag and Senator McMaster, he had considered leaving the job that had given him so much and had taken even more. His reenlistment term had come up recently, and Shane had actually put in to leave the military, rather than stay just a few more years to retire. He'd figured out that he wasn't the kind of man this new force needed.

So, technically, he wasn't AWOL. But it was a murky thing. Montag was working on dangerous and highly illegal projects that he couldn't show anyone else within the ranks. Shane hadn't even been privy to it since Montag had figured Shane for a whistleblower. Montag had been right.

So Montag and the others couldn't report Shane missing because, technically, he'd been missing at first *because* of Montag's projects. Shane hadn't known it at the time, but every mission he'd been on for the past year hadn't been ordered by anyone but Montag, who was now apparently going rogue.

Everything Shane had worked for was gone. Everything he had believed in, shattered.

So now, Shane had a choice: learn to live once again as the man he'd become, the wolf he was becoming, or give up.

And Shane Bruins did not give up. Ever.

According to Gideon and the others, he was Pack now so he would have to live under Pack law rather than human law. Only now that the humans knew about the wolves, would things change once again? Shane didn't know the answer to that, and honestly, thinking about it too hard hurt his brain. So instead, he pushed those thoughts aside and vowed to himself that he'd fight for what was right. And that meant he'd fight for the Pack that had taken him in when he'd had nowhere else to go. So he'd work with the Pack, learn who he was once again, and hopefully find a way to have the wolves and humans work together as one, rather than apart.

The thing was, Shane knew the vast majority of the human population didn't care and weren't scared. There were activist groups proudly accepting the existence of the things that went bump in the night. It seemed to Shane that it was the vocal minority who were against the shifters, as well as key players in Washington that wanted to use this new reveal to their advantage.

Well, Shane would just have to do his best to make sure that didn't happen.

He took a deep breath, trying to relieve some of the tension in his shoulders, but he couldn't quite make that work. His body didn't hurt as much as it had the day he'd showed up on the Talons' doorstep, nor did it hurt as much as it had in the days after, but he still wasn't up to the level he'd been when he was human.

Human.

How strange that he was now thinking of himself as something other than human. Though the others swore they scented wolf on him, he wasn't sure they were telling the full truth. They wanted to wait and see how he would react to the full moon. And because he was the first of his kind, he didn't blame their hesitance when it came to trusting him and what he would turn into. He didn't know either.

He wasn't human anymore, nor did he know if he was wolf. He was somewhere in between, and that worried him just as much as the fact that there were two wolves out there that made him want more.

"How are you feeling?"

Shane turned on his heel at the sound of Gideon's voice and fisted his hands at his sides. He hadn't heard his Alpha approach. Shane had been standing in the middle of his new house, but he'd left the door open, needing to air it out as it had been empty for a year or two. For such a large man, Gideon could sure move quietly. And though there had been *something* inside Shane that he could now recognize as a bond, or perhaps a sense of awareness of the nearness of Gideon, he couldn't decipher it yet. They'd told him that would come with time and practice, but they'd been saying that about everything.

"Like I'm lost," Shane said honestly, surprising himself. Since he'd already started, he might as well tell Gideon most of it. "I feel edgy. Like I don't quite fit under my skin."

Gideon nodded. "Come with me."

Shane raised a brow. "Where?"

Gideon snorted. "You know, most people would just come with me. I *am* Alpha, after all."

Shane shook his head. "You're not a dictator, that much I can tell. Maybe those who would come with you without question know you inside and out and figure you have a reason. But you still allow others to question you."

The other man tilted his head, studying him, so much like a wolf that Shane had to blink. "Perhaps. Now follow me. We're going to take a walk into the forest so you can feel the wind on your face and the den's magic on your skin. You're edgy as hell, so if you don't want to come with me, I'll make it an order with the force of my Alpha wolf behind it. You need the walk."

The order bristled Shane, though it shouldn't have. He'd been taking orders his entire life. Though the recent ones had all been lies. Perhaps that's why Gideon's order just then made him want to be surly.

"Don't even try it," Gideon growled. "I know it sticks in your craw that you have to listen to me after your last leader fucked you over, but you'll get over it. You're not at full strength yet, and you need the connection to the Pack. So get a move on."

With that, Gideon turned around and headed out, as if knowing Shane would follow. Much to Shane's chagrin, he did indeed follow soon after, closing the door behind him. They'd put his hand up to the scanner when they'd shown him the place, so now it would only unlock for him or one of the ruling members of the Pack in an emergency.

He had a home now.

And maybe he should start fighting for it.

Shane hurried his pace to catch up to Gideon, and soon, the two of them were jogging peacefully through the woods. He didn't know if it was just being near a wolf of such immense strength or the forest itself, but Shane could feel himself relax a bit. It wasn't like it was when Bram or Charlotte were around, but it was something, at least.

The stopped by a cool stream and each drank some water before resting alongside a large rock.

"Why did that help me?" he asked.

Gideon looked over at him. "Because we're not human. Not fully anyway. We have wolf counterparts within our bodies. For those of us who are born wolves, that connection is always there and always will be. We don't start being able to shift. That comes when we are two or three, sometimes earlier, sometimes later, but we're still wolves in human form. That's what scares some of the humans who are against us. That and a few other things. But though we're wolves, we also have human halves that give us the ability to reason and to live like we do. We try to find peace, and we had for a long time before the Unveiling. I hope we can find that peace again in my lifetime."

Since wolves apparently lived for hundreds of years, that was quite a statement.

"With wolves who are changed, things are slightly different, but not forever. They have to learn how to live with another...being within them. They need to control the wolf, to allow the moon goddess to tighten and strengthen the bonds. They need to *believe*. Not only do they now have the ability to shift into another form, they also have to fight the instincts they had as humans and learn to live in a new type of societal structure. There are submissive wolves, maternal ones, dominants, and those in the higher powers with gifts from the moon goddess and even more bonds to the Pack like my family. It takes time, and we are constantly evolving and changing as we learn and grow, but eventually, a Pack can lead to calm, to peace."

Shane listened, learning, soaking in as much information as he could. "But I'm not either of those things."

Gideon nodded, a frown on his face. "No, you aren't. Montag's people created a serum that somehow mimics what a bite from an Alpha or a *very* dominant wolf can do. Not every wolf can change a human into a shifter, and not every human is able to change at all. It usually takes that human being near death and getting multiple bites from a specific wolf for a change to occur. You almost died, for sure, and now you carry the scent of a wolf along your skin, but we won't know what will happen to you on a full moon. The moon is coming, and we'll be here to help you if you do change."

"If," Shane whispered. "That's a big if."

Gideon nodded. "Yeah, it is. And that's one reason why some within the Pack aren't fully ready to accept you." He shook his head. "Our Pack isn't as healthy as the Redwoods. We went through hell during my father's time as Alpha, and it's taken years to get where we are now. Those that opposed me as Alpha are mostly gone either because they left for other Packs or became lone wolves." He paused. "Others fought and lost." He pinched the bridge of his nose. "I hate that, you know. I hate that I had to fight wolves that I knew since I was a boy because they'd rather have a tyrant as a leader than me. But I fought. And yet there are still those that hold a sliver of distrust or resentment. The moon goddess chose me as Alpha, but I still had to fight for the right. Some believe I didn't fight hard enough. Some believe the moon goddess chose wrong. But when the time comes, and you need to shift into a wolf, we will stand by your side and help you. You saved my brother, and for that, I can never repay you. However, I can at least do this."

Shane listened to the Alpha bare a part of him Shane wasn't sure he let many others see. He didn't know why Gideon was telling him such personal things, but he knew it was a gift in and of itself. He wouldn't take that for granted.

"I want to help more," Shane said. "And I have an idea if you'll listen." Something had been percolating in the back of his mind.

Gideon's eyes brightened. "Good." He got up and stretched. "Then come with me to my house. The others are gathering there for a meeting, and you can tell them all." He nodded. "After you tell me on the way, of course."

Shane held back a snort at the order. Once an Alpha, always an Alpha.

When they made it to Gideon's home, Shane's wolf, or whatever it was, had pushed him close to the edge once again. The walk with the other man had helped, but it hadn't been a permanent solution.

It probably didn't help that so many wolves were inside Gideon's home. It would probably make anyone who wasn't used to the amount of sheer power unnerved. Gideon was there, of course, and his pregnant mate, Brie. The Beta of the Pack, Mitchell, stood with his back to the wall next to the Enforcer, Kameron. Ryder, the Heir, and his mate Leah sat on one couch next to Brandon, the Omega. Walker, the Healer, lazed in an armchair, while Max lay on the floor next to him. Though it was mostly Talons in the room, the Redwoods were on the large computer screens someone had set up, and Bram and Charlotte were on the other couch in the room. He figured those two were there to help him, and, while he was still confused, he was grateful.

"Take a seat," Gideon ordered.

Brie rolled her eyes. "Nice to see you," she added, and Gideon let out a little growl.

Shane gave a small smile and took the only seat left in the room—the one next to Charlotte. He figured there was a reason everyone had left that space, including Max, who had taken a spot on the floor, but he wouldn't ask about it now. First, he had to lay out his plan, and then he could deal with the other things. He used to be better at multi-tasking, but that had been before a crazed man had stuck a syringe full of poison in his vein.

He sat down next to Charlotte, their thighs touching, and he did his best to ignore the way her mouth parted at the contact. He met Bram's eyes over Charlotte's head and saw a heat in them he didn't understand. Were the two of them together and Shane was too close? He wasn't sure, but he knew he had to worry about that later, not now.

"So, what do you have planned for us?" Mitchell asked, pulling Shane from his dangerous thoughts. The other man frowned at Shane, but he didn't take it personally. Mitchell seemed to frown at everyone.

"If there are others worried about *how* I became what I am and frankly, what I could become, then why don't we find a way to make sure that can't happen again?"

Gideon nodded. The other man knew what Shane was going to say, and Shane was grateful the Alpha had looked interested on the walk over.

"What do you have in mind?" Ryder asked, his voice a little quieter than the others. He had his arm around his mate's shoulders, a content look on his face that seemed a little new to Shane. He didn't know the man other than what he'd seen in the news with the twenty-four-hour coverage of the Packs, but he knew Ryder's mating was new and hard-fought.

"Now that I can actually think again and can stay awake for longer than an hour at a time, I can remember where I was taken and where Montag injected me." Shane didn't look at the other two on the couch since he figured they knew they were the reason for his ability to think at all.

Mitchell leaned forward. "You can find the building?"

Shane nodded before frowning. "They caught me getting Ryder out of the other building and took me to this one a few miles away that I hadn't known existed. I heard others around me, but I don't know if they'll still be there." He met the others' gazes, one by one. "They could have been wolves or even humans Montag wanted to inject the serum into. Either way, they were there, and we might be able to help them now that I can remember where to go." He sighed. "I regret that it took me this long."

Charlotte reached out and took his hand. The contact sent a shock through his arm, but he didn't pull away. "You needed to heal first. We understand that." Though she wasn't a Talon, she looked at the others with her brow raised, and they nodded slowly.

Fierce.

"I remember seeing a container where Montag kept the other injections, as well. The General was saying to the others that they only had this one batch since it was so new and they wanted to try some...experiments first. He also said that there was only one place their formula was located. That way, others couldn't get their hands on it before it was perfected for his own use."

"Why did he say these things around you?" Brandon asked, his face serious. "He didn't lay out his entire plan, but it seems he laid out a lot."

"He didn't expect that you'd live long enough to do anything about it," Bram bit out, and Shane nodded.

"If it hadn't been for Gideon taking me in, I know I would have died," Shane said after a moment. "Whatever they had in that vial didn't work completely. It took an Alpha letting me into a Pack for anything to happen. So what they have isn't viable, but it's still there. We need to get rid of it, and once we do, maybe the others can sleep easier."

Gideon ran a hand over his beard. "That may be the case, but there will still be issues as the formula could be found in your blood."

"Maybe, maybe not," Walker put in. "With the bonds you put in place, it could be that it's nothing like what it was when it first started. I've been studying what I can because we need to know, but I honestly don't think anyone would be able to get anything out of what is in Shane's veins."

"Then we need to make sure the Pack knows that," Brie said then held up a hand. "Maybe not right away, but when and if you guys take out this building and destroy the samples, the Pack needs to know we're thinking of *all* outcomes."

Shane admired the strength Brie held in her voice. She was such a small woman among a group of large wolves. She might be a submissive wolf, but she'd mated one hell of a dominant Alpha. Brie Brentwood was a wolf you wanted on your side.

"Then let's make a plan," Gideon said next.

And they did, along with the Redwoods, who had been quiet during the initial part but now voiced their opinions and goals. It wouldn't be easy, Shane knew, and the way they worked as one, as wolves, was unlike anything he'd ever been a part of, but now that he was Pack, he knew he wouldn't have it any other way. If he could give these people even this much, maybe that would show the others he wasn't the enemy.

Now he just had to believe it himself.

As the group dispersed, plans in place and a scheme ready to be implemented the next day, Shane left the others to talk Pack business. They were the ruling family and had more responsibilities than he'd thought.

Bram and Charlotte came with him, as well. Since they were Redwoods, it made sense that they wouldn't be needed for the rest of the meeting. His body relaxed as they walked, just the mere presence of these two helped him in more ways than he ever thought possible.

When they reached a small patch of grass between some large trees, he stopped and turned toward them. He'd been quiet long enough, and now that he'd spoken to the Brentwoods, he needed to get this off his chest, too.

"I can't take it anymore," Shane bit out. "Why? Why can you two help me calm down so I can think? Why do the two of you give me so much control over something I've never had before? And why...why do I feel such a connection, a pull toward the two of you? I just don't get it."

Bram clenched his jaw, but it was Charlotte who spoke, her dark eyes wide, earnest. "You feel this connection because we feel it, too. The three of us...we could be mates."

Shane took a step back, stunned. "What does that mean?"

"It means we have the potential to be mates. Not just two of us, but all three of us. In a true triad." She bit her lip, looking sexy as hell. "At least, that's what I think anyway. I just don't know, but this isn't the time to talk about it. Bram and I need to head back to our den, and you need to rest so we can all go and hunt tomorrow. Our Packs' futures rests on our shoulders, and I know you want to talk more about what could be, what is so confusing, but that has to wait." She let out a shaky breath. "We need to put our Packs first just this once."

Shane's mind whirled. Mates? Triad? The *three* of them? Holy hell. He couldn't think. Couldn't breathe. And because he couldn't formulate words, Charlotte's need to worry about the Pack first sounded like a hell of a good idea.

Bram was still silent, but there was so much emotion, so much depth in his eyes, that Shane knew he wasn't just ignoring them. He was reeling, too.

Charlotte threw up her hands and cursed. "I didn't mean to blurt that out like that. Let's just save the world first, then we'll deal with whatever the hell is going on. Okay?"

Shane gave a hollow laugh at that. "Okay," he said after a moment. "Okay."

Bram just shook his head, a small smile on his face. "Saving the world it is."

And that's when Shane knew nothing would ever be the same, no matter how hard he tried. Because the idea that saving the world right then could be an easier task than whatever would go on between the three of them spoke volumes.

Saving the world, Shane thought. Yeah, they would have to do that first.

Then maybe, just maybe, he could save himself.

CHAPTER SEVEN

What had she been thinking? Charlotte *hadn't* been thinking, that was for sure. She'd blurted out the words she should have held closer for just a little bit longer, and now she wasn't sure what she was going to do. She hadn't even talked to Bram about it, and yet had felt the need to tell Shane when neither of them was ready for something like that.

She'd been selfish by putting her own needs, her own wolf, ahead of the major operation that was about to take place. That wasn't like her in any shape or form. She'd always put her Pack, her family, first. And yet she hadn't been able to hold back the truth.

If it had been any other person with either Pack, they would have already known why there was that tension between the three of them. Maybe they weren't a triad, but there *was* something going on, and if Shane had known what to do with the wolf inside him, he would have caught on. He was going through so much, she knew, and apparently, something deep inside hadn't wanted her to go through any more. Keeping secrets only hurt people in the end, and yet she'd wanted to hold back just a bit longer.

She didn't know what she was going to do for herself, let alone how the others would react. She'd already tried mating with someone, already given over to the need that had coursed through her. It hadn't worked, damn it. She'd failed at a process so inherent to the needs of shifters that her kind went willingly into fate's hands and trusted the moon goddess ninety percent of the time. Most people didn't reject their potential mates, as there was a *reason* the moon goddess put them together. Their human halves fell in love and knew without a doubt that the other person was the other half of their soul.

Though she'd known it was a risk to Bram to be mated to her considering where she'd come from, she'd fully given in. And had been rejected. Not by Bram, but by fate itself.

And now, the moon goddess was giving her a second chance. Perhaps even a third. Only she wasn't sure she was worthy enough for the two men who could be hers. She knew the blood that flowed in her veins. The man who had fathered her had murdered hundreds and sacrificed his own daughter to bring a demon into the world. That man's son had also killed and tortured hundreds of wolves and humans in his own right, his sense of decency long since diluted by the blood of the innocent.

How could the moon goddess want to gift Charlotte with a mate and a future when her family had caused so much hurt to the world around her?

Yes, Ellie had found a mate with Maddox, but Ellie had been through a far greater hell than Charlotte had. She'd paid the penance for the cruel men's sins, and yet Charlotte didn't feel she had yet. Yes, she'd been taken from her birth mother at a young age and forced to live in a basement, chained to a wall and forever encased in silence, but she didn't think it was enough. It would never be enough. Countless men and women had died because of the Centrals' Alpha's greed and cruelty, and Charlotte would never be able to wash that away.

But now it seemed she had a choice. So many choices. Bram or Shane. Bram *and* Shane.

And because she hadn't been able to help herself, she'd told Shane the real reason she and Bram could calm his wolf. Because he'd been born human, she wasn't sure he got the full scope of what it all meant. She couldn't wrap her head around it herself.

Charlotte ran a hand over her face and sighed. She needed to shower quickly and head back to the Talons so they could do what they needed to do. She didn't have time to keep her head in the clouds and worry about things out of her hands. She would go with the others to the compound and do what she did best— move *fast*. She was one of the fastest wolves in the Pack, and she'd use that to her advantage.

And when they were done, maybe, just maybe, she'd sit down with Bram and Shane again and worry about everything else. But right now, she couldn't think of the personal things in her life, only the Pack's future.

She quickly stripped out of her clothes and turned on the shower. The water heated quickly, and she slid under the spray, letting out a long sigh of pleasure at the sensation of the hot water on her skin. She'd always loved hot showers, much to her family's chagrin since she'd had to share the bathroom with her two younger sisters. Maybe it was because she hadn't had long or hot showers at all when she'd been a child that she took this one form of pleasure when she could.

What most people didn't know about the Pack she'd grown up in was that the Centrals weren't always like that. In fact, they'd been a strong and valiant Pack much like the Redwoods before her father had broken something deep inside himself to become who he'd become. And because there had been decent people left within the Pack, who had seen what their den was becoming, they'd left, hidden within the forest and created their own version of a Pack. They didn't have an Alpha or anything the moon goddess would have gifted them with, but they had been taint free of the disease that had spread throughout the rest of the Centrals. They didn't have hot showers, and they lived under the radar for as long as they could. Charlotte's mother had been one of those deserters, doing everything she could to protect her daughter from a Pack that would see her destroyed. Though Charlotte knew the distance between her mother and her mate, the Alpha, was what had eventually killed her, Charlotte had never been as proud of a person as she was her mother.

The fact that she had that woman's blood running through her veins was the only reason she had any semblance of hope most days.

She hadn't thought about her birth mother in a long while. It hurt too much most days, and Ellie had been the best kind of mother, everything Charlotte had ever needed. She didn't like looking into the past, and she had been a lot recently. She knew it was probably because she was worried about what the future would bring.

Honestly, she wasn't sure what she was going to do about Shane and Bram. Maybe it would be best...maybe it would be best if the two of them mated and she stood aside. Maybe they would be happier without a woman like her near them.

She quickly wiped away the tears that dared to fall and finished showering. There was no use crying over something she wasn't going to deal with right now. First, she had to save her people from whatever schemes this Montag had and get rid of the poison that had made Shane into what he was.

Then she could deal with her own crap.

And that was the seventh time she'd told herself that, so maybe it was time she actually did it instead of just talking about it. She turned off the shower and dried off, her mind finally on the mission at hand. Once she was dressed and her hair back in a braid, she stretched her arms over her head, centering herself for what was to come.

She'd been lost for so long, even when others thought she was finally found. Tonight, however, she had a purpose, a plan. She would work with her Pack and the Talons to ensure there was a future for her people. One free of the dangerous propositions Montag and the others held so close to their chests.

She was wolf first, woman second tonight.

And she would fight.

Shane's presence by her side heated her from the inside out, but her wolf didn't push her to move closer. In fact, it seemed to steady at the idea of being so close to Shane on one side and Bram on the other.

Tonight they had a mission, and her wolf was eagerly waiting to show off her skills. That, Charlotte thought with a smile, was satisfying.

The wolves were strategically placed around the compound in human form. If needed, they would shift, but it would be better to not tip anyone off to their presence. And seeing wolves around this particular area would do just that. Though Shane wasn't a hundred percent yet, they needed him there in case there were any details he'd missed when he'd briefed them. With so many things going on, it wouldn't surprise Charlotte if he had. He'd been drugged and out of his mind the last time he'd been here, after all. They'd placed Charlotte and Bram with him to keep him steady, and while she'd thought that would have made it more difficult for her, it had just the opposite effect. Her wolf *needed* to know where these two were, and because they didn't have a bond to aid in that, their physical closeness would have to do.

She inhaled deeply, ignoring the two scents around her as they wove together to form an intricately enticing aroma, and studied the landscape around her. Bram was to her left, Shane to her right, and she did her best not to think about how perfect it felt. They would have to talk soon, she knew, because it was getting harder and harder to focus on the more important things.

Her senses told her there were at least ten guards stationed around the compound, but she couldn't tell if anyone was *inside* the building. Either it was an empty husk, and the guards were there to protect the equipment or even act as a decoy, or there was something blocking her. Knowing these particular humans as she did, she wouldn't put any of those scenarios past them.

Bram leaned close, his body pressed tightly against hers, the warmth of his breath on her neck doing horrible things to her self-control. "We're going in soon. You ready?" His voice was so low that she could barely hear it, and his lips were at her ear.

She nodded. Her wolf was beyond ready. The men and women behind the horrors that Shane had described needed to be dealt with. It shouldn't be wolf against human, human against human, or even wolf against wolf. It was always those who broke the laws of nature against those who fought for the health and safety of the rest of them.

She leaned into Shane then, and he lowered his head so she could speak to him. "Ready?"

He nodded, and though it was dark, her eyes were wolf, and she could see him clearly.

The Alphas moved first and went in. She followed, the men at her side. They didn't need her speed yet, and she wasn't sure they would at all, but for now, they needed quiet. If they *did* need her talents, she would be ready.

Each set of wolves took out a guard; doing their best to be so silent that not even Charlotte could hear them work. The three of them took out the closest guard as a team. Though they'd never worked together like this, it was as if they had been born to do it.

Bram came up behind the man, covering his mouth with his hand while wrapping his arm around his neck. Charlotte took care of the man's weapons before he could use them, and Shane tied the man up, even as Bram continued to hold him down, eventually causing the man to lose consciousness. They wouldn't kill unless they had to. They weren't on den lands or even near the wards, and the Alphas had wanted to make sure they didn't leave a trail of bodies for the press to find.

They left the man alone, tied up, unconscious, and free of weapons and any way to communicate, and put him far enough away that it would be hard for anyone to see him—and where he'd be relatively safe from what they were about to do.

The wolves had plans tonight, and they weren't going to let this guard get in the way.

Charlotte noted that the man hadn't been military and frowned. Apparently, Shane had been correct, and Montag had officially gone off the rails. This wasn't going to end well in the long run, she figured, but first, she had to see what was inside this building.

She still couldn't sense anyone inside, and was afraid they might be too late for whoever had been imprisoned here as Shane was. They crept inside, on alert. They were armed with claws and guns, well trained in using both. Though the wolf inside sneered at the thought of using a weapon other than herself, Charlotte lived in the real world and would do what she needed to in order to protect her Pack.

The place was as silent as a tomb.

Empty.

She shook her head, sadness creeping up inside her as they viewed an empty cage.

"They kept wolves here," Bram growled low. There was no one inside the building except for her people, so they were allowed to speak now. Bram had even swept the place for bugs, but even that had come up empty. Whoever had been in this place had truly left everything behind as they'd fled.

Well, not everything.

"I know," she said finally. "I don't scent any new blood." She winced. "Only old."

Shane frowned at Charlotte's side. "Is that what I'm smelling?" He rubbed his temple. "Everything is so much stronger than it was before. Scents, sounds...everything. It wasn't even this bad at the den."

Charlotte turned to him, studying the lines that had formed on his brow. "We're getting closer to the full moon. What you're sensing is what we do every day. You'll learn to live with it, I promise. And you'll even learn to pick out different scents and sounds while drowning out the others like white noise. We'll help you." She paused. "If you want," she added.

"I think that would be a good idea," Shane said after a moment. He ran a hand over his muscled forearm and frowned. "My skin even hurts right now. Hell, this is going to take some getting used to."

Bram snorted. "You can say that much. We'll get you through, though. But first, let's do another sweep because we need to find those vials."

Charlotte cursed herself. Once again, she'd gotten stuck on other problems rather than the one at hand. She just couldn't bear seeing Shane hurting, much like she couldn't bear seeing Bram as frustrated as he was right then.

"The cages are empty," she said again, her voice hollow. "Do you think they took whoever was in them when they left?"

Bram's gaze went stony. "I don't know, Char. I don't even know which would be the better answer."

"If Montag took them with him, they're as good as dead," Shane growled. "He was always a fierce leader, but I never knew he was a cruel one until it was too late."

What would it feel like to know everything you'd fought for had been part of a lie? Charlotte wondered. Well, not everything for sure, but so many of Shane's recent missions had been for Montag. And though she'd called him the enemy when she'd first found out about him, she knew she'd been wrong. There was no way a man could have that bleakness in his eyes at the sight of what his former commander had done and be part of the problem in the first place. Shane was the solution now, and Charlotte could only be grateful for that.

"We need to keep moving," Bram said after a moment. If she hadn't known him as long as she had, she'd have thought his words cold, but she could hear the underlying pain and rage warring within him. It did none of them any good to stand here and go through the thousands of different possibilities and outcomes of those within the cages. They had a job to do, and they needed to get on that.

The three of them met up with the others who had found more cages and exam rooms. Charlotte held back a shudder at the memories that came at her. She'd been in a building much like this one before, but she hadn't been in the same position as she was now. She was far stronger now. She was free. She needed to remember that.

Shane pinched the bridge of his nose before shaking his head. "I think the room they kept me in is this way. It's all a blur, but I'm getting fragments when I walk around and try to place things."

She followed him, praying all of this hadn't been a waste of time and energy. Not only did their Packs need a boost, but she figured Shane did, as well. If people were afraid of what his existence meant within the Pack, not knowing if there were more like him would only put more of a target on Shane's back. Those people who were at wit's end needed a place to put their anger and frustration, their fears and uncertainties. It seemed like Shane was the easy choice for now, and Charlotte didn't want him hurt in the melee.

She followed Shane with Bram at her side, her senses on alert. The place had been empty a few days, it felt like, but there *had* been guards outside. Just what were they protecting?

When Shane stopped in front of a door and put his hand on the butt of his gun, Charlotte tensed. One day soon, he'd learn to use his claws, not the weapon first. During a fight, wolves were usually faster than the bullets that came at them. And if they were hit, they could still move through the pain and heal, even if it wasn't easy.

"This is it," Shane said in a low voice. "This is where they kept me and where I last saw the vials. The computer is in here, too, and Montag said it wasn't connected to a network so others wouldn't be able to steal the formula."

"If it's still here, then we at least have something," Bram added. "Do you want me to go in first?"

Charlotte looked between the two men, a charged spark of silence blooming between them.

Shane shook his head. "I can do it."

He opened the door, and they followed him. When he let out a relieved sigh, Charlotte's wolf pushed at her, wanting to be closer.

Not yet, she reminded her wolf. *Maybe not ever.*

Gideon followed her into the room with a frown on his face. "Is it here?" he asked, his voice a growl, but she could tell his wolf wasn't up front yet. He was just *that* dominant.

Shane nodded and pointed toward a large box on a counter. "That's the case where the vials were I think." He tilted his head toward another counter. "And the computer is still here."

Charlotte moved past all of them and inhaled, using her senses to see if anything was amiss. She couldn't scent any traps or extra security measures, but she would be careful when she opened the case anyway.

She slowly lifted the lid and swallowed hard. "They're still here."

Nineteen vials of poison neatly tucked away with one empty place where someone had used one. The one that had changed Shane's life forever.

Bram came to her side and looked down. "So much power in one tiny vial."

"So much hate," she added in a whisper.

"It doesn't work, though," Shane added in from behind them. "I needed Gideon's help, remember?"

Charlotte looked over her shoulder at him. "You're right, but since there *is* a way still..."

"Destroy it," Shane bit out. "It's dangerous in any hands, even ours."

Gideon nodded. "That's the plan. We're not even going to take one to study. That's how bad decisions are made, and things end up in the wrong hands."

"I'm looking over the computer now, and the formula is still here, *and* it looks like it's still not connected to a network," Max said from behind them. Charlotte had been aware others had entered the room, but she'd been focused on the vials at the time.

"We're destroying that, too," Gideon ordered. "We want no evidence of what they did here."

Kameron rolled his shoulders and met Charlotte's gaze for a moment before turning to his brother, their Alpha. "We'll set the majority of the charges here and put the rest at key places to ensure the explosion doesn't harm any of the outlying areas. If you guys want to get out and give me and my people some space to work, we'll be ready shortly."

Charlotte suppressed a shiver. Kameron was always so cool, remote, in all of his deals. At first, she had thought it was because he was the Enforcer and that was his role, but now she wasn't so sure. There was something lurking beneath the surface she didn't quite understand.

In the end, though, she ignored it, knowing he was loyal and dedicated to his Pack, even if he scared her. She made her way outside the building. She was still on alert since anyone could be watching, but they had other wolves around the perimeter for that reason. The world wasn't that large anymore with so many people looking in on what shifters were doing at all times, but for now, she felt as if in the darkness here, she could be alone...or at least hidden amongst the shadows.

"You think it'll be over once the building is gone?" Shane asked after a few minutes of silence.

She stood once again between Bram and Shane. Bram, she knew, always tried to protect her, even if it was the simple task of standing near, but now Shane seemed to be doing it instinctually, as well. Soon, she'd have to teach Bram once more and Shane for the first time just how strong of a wolf she was. But for now, she let them work their protection gig.

They'd learn soon enough.

The first explosion rocked the ground beneath them, but they didn't stagger. They'd been expecting it, after all. All of the wolves were a safe distance away. Kameron and his people were fast and efficient—they wouldn't be working with the Enforcer if they weren't.

"No," she answered as flames escaped the windows and the structure collapsed in on itself. "No, I think it's only the beginning."

What came next was a mystery, but Charlotte prayed they were strong enough to face it.

COLLECTION

General Montag watched the monitors as his original compound burned to ash. He fisted his hands at his sides and cursed.

Damn wolves.

They'd found his research and had destroyed it. He hadn't had time to grab everything on his way out. He might have tried to keep the computer on him as well as a vial or two, but he hadn't been able to ensure its safety. He'd had meetings in Washington, and couldn't have ensured the security it would take to keep his secrets hidden. Senator McMaster was already too suspicious of everything he was doing, even if the other man was supposedly on his side.

He'd never had cameras inside the building where he'd kept his plans, as he hadn't wanted his face on anything that would incriminate him. However, he'd had a few placed outside the compound for an extra layer of security. He was glad he had because the men he'd hired had been useless. When he'd found out just how useless, he'd had them silenced permanently. There were no second chances when it came to a future of his making.

Montag paused the screen and looked at the image there. He'd thought Bruins dead, but he'd been wrong. The man was alive and *working* with the wolves. If anything, he seemed stronger, more alert.

The serum had worked.

Montag gripped the edge of his desk. And because of his need for secrecy, he'd lost everything it had taken to make the formula.

He touched the screen, his fingertip tracing Shane's face. Not everything. The formula lay within the ex-soldier's veins. Now that he knew Shane was alive, he'd find him and take him. There was no other option with so much on the line.

Montag's attention turned to the dark-haired woman at Shane's side and the other man in the frame. These two had worked with Shane and leaned toward him in other images. That fact might be useful later. Just what hedonistic things was Shane up to in the animal den?

As he clenched his jaw, Montag started working on a new plan. If Shane was alive and indeed a wolf, that meant he needed to be in the right hands. Not those of an animal who thought itself a leader. They called themselves Packs and howled at the moon like the dirty dogs they were. He didn't care for what they turned into, but he did care what their strength could do for him.

He would be invincible with an army of wolves that only knew him as their leader.

There would be no more loss of human life, no more endless wars where he had the possibility of losing.

He would be their savior.

People would remember his name, his duty, his purpose.

He would be immortal.

And he only needed Shane Bruins to do it.

CHAPTER EIGHT

Things had been easier when he'd only been in love with his best friend. At least then, he only had one thing to worry about. Now it seemed as if the entire world had thrown him for a loop, and he wasn't sure he'd find his footing again.

Someone slammed into his side, and he fell on his ass. He growled and tried to get back on his feet—much like he was already trying to do mentally—and hit the ground again when Kameron pushed him down.

"I'll still always win," Kameron said. The man grinned as he said it, but it didn't reach his eyes. Bram could never quite figure out this wolf, but he supposed it wasn't his place to do so. He wasn't even a Talon member.

Bram flipped the Enforcer off before pushing back, using a little more force than usual, but not enough to draw attention to him. Kameron's eyes narrowed as he found himself on his back with Bram standing over him. Bram just shrugged and went back to the game.

Even though they were still on high alert since they'd taken out Montag's buildings, the wolves needed to do something to relieve the tension. Those with mates could at least work out the rising anxiety the old-fashioned way. Those without mates either found a willing body they could at least have a physical relationship with without being mates, or did what Bram was doing.

Work it out another way.

In his case, it was the Redwood and Talon monthly football matches. They played by wolf rules and used every advantage they could short of bloodshed to score. Last time, they'd played in the Redwood den, and the Talons who weren't on duty had come over to play a decent game. Bram's team had won, of course, since he and Charlotte had kicked Kameron's and Brandon's asses. This time, they were on Talon territory, not only working out the tension that came from being on alert all the time, but also strengthening the bonds between the Packs. Just because the Packs were allies, didn't mean there weren't problems. So games like this where they could beat up on each other innocently helped.

It wasn't a completely civilized answer to a non-civilized problem, but they weren't human.

They were wolves.

And they were physical.

Of course, that thought brought in another thought of just how he, Shane, and Charlotte could be physical after this, and that just brought his wolf that much closer to the edge. They were days from the full moon, and everyone was much more wolf. Even though Bram was perpetually closer to his wolf, he usually had tight control of it. His proximity to not one, but *two* of his mates made it a little harder for him. He knew Charlotte had been running each night, trying to work out the extra energy she had, and Shane was getting grumpier by the day.

There were other ways the three of them could work this out, but Bram knew this wasn't the time. *After the game*, he promised himself. After the game, the three of them would sit down and talk. It had only been two days since Charlotte had revealed what they were, or rather, what they could be to Shane, and they hadn't taken the time to fully explain it to the man. The responsibility lay on Charlotte's and Bram's shoulders since the other man hadn't grown up with wolves and didn't know anything about mating. They could have talked about it this morning rather than him and Charlotte playing this game while Shane watched, but Bram had needed to run off some of his excess energy.

Charlotte, he could see, needed to, as well. They always had her play wide receiver because she could run faster than most of the others if she put her mind to it. She just had to get past the wall of wolves, and Kade or Finn could throw the ball to her. Bram held back a snort. *Of course,* the Alpha and Heir were playing QB. As if either of them would give up control to play any other position nowadays.

As Gideon was the Talon QB, Bram figured it was an Alpha thing.

Kade was back at the den so the younger Jamenson was playing leader today and Finn called out another play. Bram rolled his shoulders and tried to get his mind in the game.

This time, it was Brandon who came at him, a small smile on his face. Bram blocked the other man from getting to Charlotte and did his best not to groan when Brandon elbowed him in the gut. These Talons weren't playing around. Parker came around Bram to take out Walker, and Brandon slid from Bram's grip.

In fact, the other man slid right down into the mud, falling on his ass. His eyes were wide, his mouth gaping like a fish before it pressed into a thin line.

Bram pushed at the man's shoulder. "You okay?" The play was still going on around them, and Bram had part of his attention on Charlotte as she ran toward the end zone. Leah, Ryder's mate, was catching up to Charlotte, but Bram didn't think the other woman would reach her. As Leah was a witch, she wasn't as fast or strong as the wolves, but Ryder apparently hadn't the heart to tell her to sit out. She wasn't allowed to use her magic, but none of the wolves were allowed to tackle her either. It was a convoluted set of rules, but they knew what they were doing. The Pack had always consisted of wolves, witches, and the occasional human.

"Touchdown!" Finn yelled and did a little dance.

Bram shook his head and held out a hand to Brandon. "Finn, never do that again."

Finn just grinned and flipped him off while his mate, Brynn, wrapped her arms around the Heir's middle. Brandon took Bram's offered hand and pulled himself up.

"Seriously," Bram whispered, "you okay?"

Brandon shook himself before nodding. "Yeah, just knocked the wind out of myself."

Bram wasn't sure how that was physically possible, but he wasn't going to argue. As the Omega, Brandon could feel the emotions of every Talon Pack member. For all Bram knew, something had happened along the Pack bonds that had caused Brandon to fall.

He let it slide as it wasn't any of his business and gave the other man a chin lift before heading over to Charlotte. He grinned at her, not able to hold back any longer.

"Good job, Char."

She smiled widely at him, though it didn't quite reach her eyes—it never did anymore. "Thanks. I got lucky there for a minute. Leah is much faster than I thought."

Bram reached out to tuck a piece of hair behind her ear, and they both froze. Deliberately, he finished what he was doing and let out a breath. Her hair was so freaking soft. He remembered exactly what it felt like when it was draped over his body as she rode him.

Seeming to know where his mind had wandered, Charlotte's eyes darkened, though a slight ring of yellow appeared around the iris, telling him her wolf was out to play.

Damn it. They needed to talk, and *soon*.

"I think the game's over," another voice said from behind him, bringing Bram out of his thoughts.

He turned and moved to make room for Shane. The other man hadn't been playing because no one was sure how strong he was yet, nor how much control he had. Shane needed a little more training and a whole lot more time with his wolf before he could even simple things like play a game of football with a bunch of werewolves.

"I guess it is," Charlotte said as she looked around the field. Bram followed her gaze and noted that people were pairing up with mates or friends, leaving the field in gales of laughter and growls. "Did we win?" she asked.

Bram shrugged. "I think so. We're usually better at keeping score."

Shane let out a rough chuckle. "Yeah, you guys won, and even though you don't kick for extra points, I'm assuming everything else is the same point system as human football?"

Bram nodded. "Yeah, same system. We used to kick for extra points but ended up losing the ball nine times out of ten because we kick it so hard. We don't even kick off anymore."

"I noticed that," Shane said, a smile on his face that didn't quite reach his eyes. "I guess everything is a little different here."

"It is," Charlotte agreed. "But you'll learn."

Shane stuffed his hands in his pockets, looking a little more lost than he had before. Bram wanted to reach out and brush the hair from the other man's face as he had with Charlotte, but he didn't think any of them were ready for that yet.

"We should find someplace quiet and talk," Bram said after a moment. "It's time, don't you think?"

Shane met Bram's gaze, warring emotions shining through so brightly that Bram couldn't fathom what the other man could be thinking right at that moment. "Come to my place," he said. "I don't get many visitors."

Bram had a feeling he didn't get *any* visitors other than those who needed something from him. What would it be like to be cut off from everything you've known your entire life and thrust into a situation where not everyone trusted you? Hell, not everyone wanted Shane alive at all. Bram fisted his hands and forced them into the pockets of his sweats so the others couldn't see.

"Let's go, then." He turned to Charlotte. "You ready?"

She licked her lips, and his dick hardened. "As I'll ever be."

"Well, this should be interesting," Shane mumbled.

Interesting indeed. Just three people who had pasts so rife with confusion and angst they could

110

barely breathe from it all, finding that they were mates but not knowing if they were a triad or just three people who could pair off. Add in the fact that one was a former human turned maybe-wolf, another a wolf with too much strength for the body it was in, and another who'd grown up chained in a basement and it made it a party.

The three of them made it to Shane's place in silence, though it wasn't as tense as Bram had figured it would be, considering they were about to talk about a future that might never come. Hell, maybe *Bram* was the tense one.

There wasn't much in the small bungalow house Walker had scrounged up for Shane. A few older pieces of furniture but nothing personal. Hell, Shane didn't *have* anything personal. He'd left it all behind when he'd come to the Talons.

Bram ran a hand over his head as he watched Charlotte look around the place, a frown on her face. Shane had his hands in his pockets, confusion and a little bit of embarrassment evident on his face.

"Is there a place we can go to get your stuff?" Bram asked suddenly. "I mean, things that are yours that you might want?"

Charlotte smiled at him while Shane's eyes widened. "We can get it for you," she added in. "I mean, this is your home now. Let's make it yours."

Shane slid his palm over the bottom half of his face, rubbing his jaw. "There're a few things in storage I can probably get. The things that were at the barracks weren't really that important to me, and I don't think I'll be getting those back anyway."

"Then we'll get your stuff from storage," Bram said simply. "Just tell us where it is."

"Because I can't get it myself," Shane added, his eyes dark. "Because I can't leave the den."

Bram sighed, but it was Charlotte who answered. "No, you can't. But it's not just you, you know. A lot of people aren't safe outside the den right now because of hate groups and people like Montag, who happen to have a lot of power behind his own version of hate. Plus, any new wolf—no matter how he or she was changed—wouldn't be allowed to leave so close to the full moon before their first transition. It's not practical, and it's not just about you. I promise they aren't singling you out, even if it feels like that. So later, we'll get your things. I'm surprised Mitchell hasn't asked it about it, honestly. It's his job as Beta to make sure the day-to-day needs of the Pack members are fulfilled."

Shane winced. "He might have mentioned it, but I blew him off." Shane sat down on the old couch, resting his forearms on his thighs. I wasn't in a good mood when he asked, and he hasn't asked again."

Bram met Charlotte's gaze. "He'll either find a way to get your things without your help, or he'll show up again and ask. He always finds a way to get what he wants."

"I'm learning that fact about a lot of the Talons now," Shane said wryly. He paused as if trying to collect his thoughts. "I never thought I'd be here, you know. I figured I'd retire or get out when my term came up like I was planning to and learn to be a civilian. Turns out, I'm learning to be something else entirely. I didn't like the idea of who I would have to become if I had stayed with Montag, but I'm still not sure who I am now."

Charlotte sat down on the coffee table in front of Shane, while Bram took a seat near the other man on the couch. "There's a lot of that going around." She licked her lips, and Bram forced himself not to stare. It wasn't easy when the mating urge was riding him so hard. "I'm sorry for blurting out the whole mate thing like I did." She blew out a breath. "It's just all so much, and I tend to either block myself from things or let it all out in unintelligible instances when I'm stressed."

Shane smiled then, and Bram once again felt the mating urge hit him. The man was handsome, sure, but when he smiled? Yeah, Bram was going to be in trouble with these two.

"I don't mind that you blurted it out," Shane said. "I'd rather know why the two of you are freaking out around me and yet calming me at the same time. So I guess this is where I ask what mating is beyond the fact that wolves call their significant others mates."

Bram shook his head. "It's much more than a significant other."

Charlotte looked at Bram for a moment, sheer need on her face before turning back to Shane. "It's a bond between two wolves, but it's not just that either. You see, within the world and over time, there are wolves, witches, and humans out there that are the, for lack of a better word, perfect match for a wolf. The moon goddess, our deity, the one who made us who we are, finds us someone who has the potential to be our soul mate, our other half. While the human part of us can reject a mating because of numerous reasons, many don't because if fate twists just the right way, that mating could bring...happiness." She wiped a tear, and Bram let out a small growl.

"What is it?" Shane asked, looking between the two of them. "What am I missing?" The other man reached out hesitantly and wiped another tear from Charlotte's face. With any other man, Bram would have torn the limb from its socket for that touch alone, but with Shane, Bram couldn't help but be pleased.

That's when Bram knew the truth.

They *were* a triad. A potential for something far greater than themselves. If it had been either or, he'd have felt more at war, torn between the two of them and would have demanded a choice. Instead, he wanted *both*. And maybe, just maybe, fate would let him have it.

"Bram and I..." Charlotte began and shook her head.

"Charlotte and I have been best friends since we were children, and she came to the Redwoods."

Shane frowned. "You weren't always a Redwood?"

Charlotte let out a short laugh. "One long story at a time, okay?"

Shane ran a hand through his hair. "I'm thinking I could spend years learning new things about the two of you and these Packs and never quite catch up."

"True," Bram said, "but I'm forever learning new things, too. It keeps things interesting when we're so long-lived."

Shane's eyes widened. "Fuck," he whispered. "I...I never really thought of that."

Charlotte reached out and gripped Shane's knee. The other man licked his lips as he looked between the two of them. "One long story at a time," she repeated. "Bram and I are friends and have been for years. You see, sometimes, the mating urge, that feeling you have in your heart and within your wolf that tells you that this other person could be your mate and everything you could ever need, takes a while to show up. We'd known each other since we were children, but our wolves waited until we were old enough to possibly handle the complex emotions that came with mating."

Shane looked between the two of them. "So you're mates, then." Disappointment clouded his features. "Then how do I fit in?"

Bram shook his head. "That's just it. We tried." His voice was deep, hollow. Charlotte didn't make a sound, and he knew she was hiding her emotions once again.

"It didn't work," Charlotte put in, her voice equally hollow. "To create a mating bond, you have to bond not only the human but also the wolf."

Bram continued, "Sex bonds the humans. Or rather, the exchange of fluids so those not ready for that step wear a condom. A mating mark, a bite on the fleshy part where the shoulder meets the neck, bonds the wolf."

Charlotte ran a hand over her neck, an unconscious gesture that had both men staring with avid hunger.

"And you tried both?" Shane asked, his voice almost a growl. "And the bond didn't work?"

Charlotte shook her head. "No. I thought...I thought the moon goddess had forsaken me."

Bram let out a curse. "And you thought it was only your fault, then? Hell, Charlotte, it could have been any number of things. I hate that you constantly blame yourself for everything."

Charlotte narrowed her eyes at him. "That's a discussion for another time."

"A discussion I'd like to have, as well," Shane added in, and Bram liked the man all the more for it. "So you're saying that the two of you couldn't create a bond, and yet I'm your mate, too?" He shook his head. "Now that's not a sentence I thought I'd ever say."

"There's a lot of things you're probably going to say now that you never thought you would before," Bram added wryly.

Shane snorted. "True."

"Anyway," Charlotte put in, "we don't know if that's the case. I mean, what if the bond doesn't work again?" Pain entered her gaze, and she blinked it away.

Damn it, Charlotte. Damn it.

"I think it didn't work the way it should have with us because we weren't complete. We didn't have our third."

Shane let out a breath. "And that would be me." He met their gazes one by one. "You're saying I'm *both* your mates. Not just with Charlotte, but with Bram, too."

Bram met the other man's gaze. "And is that going to be a problem?" Bram had always been bisexual, but that didn't mean Shane was.

Shane frowned. "I'm attracted to both of you. With my previous employment, I was never in a serious relationship that lasted long enough to count, but I've been with both men and women. That's not what I'm talking about."

"You're talking about the fact that *we're* talking about three people in one relationship," Charlotte said. "In other Packs, there are triads." She looked over at Bram. "I looked it up." She met Shane's gaze again. "And my aunt and uncles are in a triad. Their bond is actually called the trinity bond, and it's a little different because it came from the moon goddess herself and was used to defeat a demon."

Shane's eyes widened, his jaw dropping. "I take it that's one of those stories you're going to have to elaborate on later."

"We'll fill you in on everything," Bram said. "But for now, we'll focus on mating. A mating bond is different than the bond you hold with your Alpha or with the Heir and Beta. It's different than the Pack bonds that create the internal structure of a Pack. They're something that is unique to each mating pair or triad. I've heard some bonds allow each wolf to find the other no matter how far apart they are. Some can even communicate telepathically across the connection."

Shane's eyes widened. "No shit?"

"No shit," Charlotte said with a small smile. "My parents have one like that actually. They don't use it too often in public or even at home when my sisters and I are around, but they still use it."

"I guess it would be weird for your parents to have a full-on conversation in their heads with you in the room," Shane said dryly.

Charlotte shrugged. "If us kids were in trouble, I guess it was helpful to make sure they were on the same page, but yeah, their bond is only for them so they use those special gifts like that on their own. Mating bonds are only for the pair or triad. They're sacred and special. Once they're made, you can't break them." She paused. "Well, I've heard of one being broken, but it almost killed those involved, and it almost created a war."

Bram shook his head. "Another story for another time," he said with a sad smile to Shane, who once again looked interested.

"I'm going to need to start taking notes," Shane put in.

"I'm sure it would help," Charlotte said honestly.

They were silent for a moment, each taking time to gather their thoughts.

"I don't know what's coming next, but what I do know is that deep inside, my wolf wants you both," Bram said softly. "That doesn't mean we should jump into bed and declare our feelings for each other or create a bond, but I do want to...I don't know, at least try to find out if this is something more than just a feeling."

Shane slid his hand through his hair again. Bram watched the way the other man's muscles worked, telling himself to calm down. He could never quite calm down in Charlotte's presence, however, and now it seemed Shane incited a similar reaction in him.

"I don't even know if I'm going to shift," Shane said softly. "I don't know what I am. *Who* I am."

"I understand," Bram said sadly, and Charlotte kept her head down, staying silent.

"No, I don't think you do," Shane whispered. "I don't know who I am, but I do know that it's time I start believing in something other than what I thought I was fighting for for so long. I want to believe in fate and something greater than me. And I *know* having the two of you around does something to me. So I have to take a chance on that. I don't know what's coming next, but I want to see what does...with the two of you." He looked at Bram then before reaching out and lifting Charlotte's chin. "Can you do that? Can you take a chance on a broken soldier who doesn't know what's inside him?"

Shane's question was so earnest that Bram reached out without thinking and put his hand on Shane's thigh. The other man tensed before relaxing. Since Charlotte had put her hand on Bram's wrist, the three were touching as one, and Bram's wolf pushed at him, wanting more.

Charlotte looked between the two men, a soft expression Bram couldn't quite read on her face. "I think that's your answer. Yes, I want to see what comes next. I just hope it doesn't break us in the process."

The relief hit Bram hard, even if the fear ebbed with it. Yes, they'd broken once before, but he'd be damned if he'd let it happen again. Everything was changing, and Bram knew they'd have to change with it or shatter again. Forever.

These two could be his future.

Maybe it was time for Bram to fight for a life worth living.

CHAPTER NINE

S hane was taking notes. He figured he'd be taking notes for the next decade at this rate and never catch up. He should have understood that changing his entire life twice over would be difficult, but he hadn't taken into account the history of a world he'd never truly been a part of.

"You're going to give yourself a brain aneurysm if you don't stop and breathe," Brandon said from his side.

The two of them were taking a walk through the den so Shane could get acquainted with the layout as well as ask any questions he could think of. Brandon was a good listener, but more importantly, when prompted, he was a good teacher. The Brentwoods had been taking turns with Shane, showing him around the den, as well as staying at either his place or one of theirs for a meal so he would feel more included.

They not only wanted him to learn what it meant to be wolf and Pack, but they also wanted the side benefit of *others* watching them. Shane hoped that if those who were wary about his presence saw him with the Alpha and his family, they might learn to trust him. Of course, trust took time, and helping them blow up one building along with the formula to create monsters wasn't enough.

Once he could shift—*if* he could shift—he'd find other ways to prove to them that he was here to stay. Honestly, he wasn't sure how he'd come to know this so quickly, as he hadn't been in the right mind when he'd shown up at the Talon's door, but he thought it probably had something to do with the bonds sliding through his system, anchoring him to a group of people he'd never met before.

Though he'd trusted his team through his career as a soldier and would have died for them if the need arose, he'd never felt what he did now. It was...different.

He stopped where he was and ran a hand over his face.

Different was the word of the day, wasn't it. And what a sad word it was since it couldn't possibly encompass everything that had happened in the past weeks.

Brandon, who had stopped walking when Shane had, merely nudged him along to a bench by a grouping of trees. The wooden seat looked like it fit perfectly with nature and not like something they'd placed without thought. He liked that about the wolves around here. They did their best not to hurt the land that fed them and always made sure it and den were taken care of.

Shane sat down slowly with Brandon taking the seat next to him. He wasn't truly in control right then since the full moon was the next day, and neither Bram nor Charlotte was there to help. Brandon, however, soothed him in a different way.

"Are you working your Omega magic on me?" Shane asked, his voice a bit rough from lack of use. He'd been doing his best to listen and learn from the other man and hadn't really spoken much that day other than to ask a question here or there.

Brandon smiled and shrugged. "Not really. It's sort of inherent sometimes, so my wolf is forever reaching out to each Pack member to see what it can do to help. Some have learned to erect shields over time to prevent my help unless I push them, and others are content enough that I don't need to help at all. There are only a few instances where I'll go out and try to do what I can with pure thought, rather than allowing my wolf to use the bonds from a distance. With you, though?" Brandon frowned. "You're a bit different, honestly."

Just what he wanted to hear. That word, different, again. Shane ran his hand over his knee, annoyed with himself for hating that word. The wolves didn't have to take him in or even like him. They didn't owe him anything. And it would do him well to remember that.

"What do you mean?"

"You're not like other wolves, Shane." The other man winced. "Sorry, that came out wrong."

Shane waved him off. "It's the truth, though. And we don't even know if I'm going to change at all. Could be, come the full moon, I'll die because I can't shift, and all of this worry will be for nothing."

The Omega pressed his lips together. "Shane, that's not what I meant, and you know we're not going to let that happen. Somehow, we're going to find a way to make this work if it doesn't happen the way it should. As for what I meant in the first place? Each wolf in this Pack is different. We aren't a damn hive mind. If there is something deep inside hurting another person, it's my job to try and fix it. With you, it's like you have a natural shield. It could go away once you shift, or it could get stronger. I don't know, but we're going to figure it out, damn it."

Shane didn't say anything in answer to that and wasn't sure there was anything he could say that would matter. He wouldn't know what the future would bring until the next night when the moon shone high in the sky and his wolf, if he indeed had one, felt the urge to shift.

"Do shifters always have to wait for the full moon for their first shift?" he asked after a moment. They'd been sitting without speaking, listening to the world around them. He could hear other Pack members talking to one another as they went about their day, as well as animals in the forest who felt safe for the moment from the predators living in their midst.

"Not at all. For those born from shifters, they can transition at any time after age two, though I know a few who shifted a during their first year." Brandon smiled then. "Startled their parents, that's for sure. The first shift for a child can come during a time of great emotion, or for those like Brie, when they feel like it's time." The other man met Shane's eyes. "According to her parents, one day she was toddling around, feeling like she needed to scratch her skin, and decided it was time to be a wolf."

"And now she's your Alpha's mate," Shane added.

"Yep, and my sister-in-law. I never would have picked a woman like her for my brother, and I'm glad I was wrong. Hell, she's the best thing that's ever happened to Gideon and our Pack."

Shane smiled then. "And now she's going to have a pup of her own." One day, he'd get used to calling children "pups" interchangeably. At least, he hoped.

"It's our first baby," Brandon said softly. "I mean, the family's first, you know? And because Brie is a submissive wolf, it'll be interesting to see what happens."

"You mean because the eldest child eventually becomes the Heir of the Pack when they're ready?"

"It doesn't always work out that way, but yes. Finn actually became the Heir at a young age because their former Alpha, Finn's grandfather, was killed during the Central war."

Shane flipped through his notes. "I don't know a lot about that time period. I was only a child then, and the humans didn't know you guys existed. It's still strange to think that all of you were fully adults at that time, too."

Brandon looked over at him, a strange expression on his face. "Not all of us. Charlotte and Bram are around your age, so they'd have been kids, too. Brie as well for that matter. Once we hit adulthood, you kind of forget that some of us have hit a century of living and still haven't lived."

Before Shane could ask the other man what he'd exactly meant by that, the Omega stood up and rubbed his chest bone.

"Hell, I need to go." He met Shane's eyes. "One of the elders needs me. Are you okay going home by yourself? I can drop you off on my way."

It wasn't a long walk, and though you could drive place to place, most walked to preserve the den's natural landscape. However, that wasn't what Shane was talking about. The others were not only worried about retaliation from Montag but also about threats *within* the Pack regarding Shane's existence. Just because they'd destroyed the samples, didn't mean it was over. Shane himself was proof that there was something out there that could change the ways of the wolves forever. And not everyone wanted him to live to become more than he already was.

Shane shook his head. "Go. Someone needs you more than I do. I'll go straight home." And didn't that grate on him. He didn't have a babysitter so he had to go home and wait.

Brandon took off with a nod, leaving Shane alone. He sat there a few more moments, taking in the sounds around him. He'd never really paid attention to nature as he had been recently. Was it because of his wolf, or because he had the time to do so now? He wasn't sure, but like with everything else lately, it was a change.

Deciding it was time to head home, he stood up but not before he heard the sounds of crunching leaves behind him. He turned, but he wasn't fast enough. Someone took out his feet while another punched him square in the face. He rocked back, the pain shooting up his face and down his spine like sharp blades sliding into his skin. Whoever it was had used the full power of their wolf. Shane wasn't wolf yet, despite how his body had changed. He was no match for these three on his own, but he'd be damned if he went out without a fight.

He punched back, getting one man in the shoulder. Shane grunted, knowing he'd probably just broken a few fingers. Hell, these guys were like solid steel, and there was no way he'd live through this without a miracle.

They got him down on the ground and on his back. Someone held his legs, while another had his arms, and the third punched him over and over. Shane yelled out but choked on his own blood.

"If you're dead, we're safe," the man on top of him grunted. "If you're dead, they can't kill us."

Shane didn't think that was the case at all as nothing could ever be that simple, but he didn't say anything. Couldn't. He tried to fight them off, but nothing worked.

He was dying.

This wasn't how he wanted to die, but hell, he'd already been close to the brink far too many times recently. But before he could take his last breath and keep fighting, the heavy weight on top of him was taken away.

Growls sounded around him, and the immense power of a strong wolf hit him like a bag of bricks to the chest. He tried to get up but he couldn't, his limbs were far too weak. Instead, he opened the one eye that hadn't swollen shut and blinked.

Bram stood above the three attackers, blood covering his forearms but other than that, not a single scratch on him. He looked powerful and...fucking hot as hell.

Probably not the best time to be thinking that, though.

"What the fuck?" Brandon yelled as he ran back to Shane's side. The Omega fell to his knees and looked down at Shane. "Holy hell. I need to call Walker. Now."

Bram growled from Shane's other side, a low rumble, dangerous, deadly, and full of promise.

"The three assholes are down for the count. I didn't kill them, but it was close." Bram flexed his hands, the claws Shane hadn't noticed initially sliding back into his fingertips. Shane wanted to learn how to do that.

He must have been wearing his thoughts on his face because both Bram and Brandon seemed to understand exactly what he was thinking.

"You'll learn," Brandon said softly, though there was heat in his eyes. "I'm going to fucking kill those idiots for doing this to you."

"You'll have to wait in line," Bram bit out. Shane watched as the other man sniffed the air. Bram seemed to be really close to his wolf at the moment. "Walker and Gideon are on their way. As are a few others. I want to know what happened and why the fuck you thought it was okay to leave Shane alone like this."

"Not. Brandon's. Fault." Shane winced with each word, and Bram shot a glare at him.

"Stop talking. You punctured your lung with a broken rib, or at least that's how it sounds."

Shane lifted a lip to mock growl, but it came out more like a wheeze. He blinked a few times, the dark spots in his vision getting larger. He passed out in pain before he could thank Bram for saving his life...again.

****

Charlotte was this close to punching someone in the face if she didn't get some answers.

"What do you mean, you left him there?" Her voice might sound calm, but she was nowhere near calm inside, and she had a feeling Brandon knew it.

The Omega's jaw tightened. "My elder needed me. It's my duty to protect those who can't protect themselves. Shane was close to his house, and should have been safe." The Omega let out a curse. "But he wasn't, and I want to rip the limbs off those bastards."

Charlotte raised a brow at the normally quiet man's words. Well okay, then.

Before Charlotte could say another word, Walker came out from Shane's bedroom, exhaustion clear on his face and blood on his pants.

Shane's blood.

Three wolves from the Talon Pack had tried to kill the man that could be her mate, and they'd nearly succeeded. The elder who had taken Brandon away from Shane's side had indeed been in pain, having opened a chest he'd thought he'd lost long ago that contained memories of his long-dead mate. The three attackers had used that fact to their advantage, having waited for just the right moment. She wouldn't know how close Shane had been to death unless Walker told her, and she wasn't sure her wolf could take the truth.

"Everything okay?" Bram asked by her side since she hadn't been able to speak.

Walker nodded slowly. "He took a beating, that's for sure. He's healing faster than he would have as a human, but not quite as quick as a wolf." He met her gaze. "That's to be expected of anyone in his position, so it's not a reflection of *how* he was changed. If it continues like this after tomorrow, well, then that's a hurdle we'll have to jump when the time comes. I also Healed him completely." The man gave a weary sigh, and she immediately went to his side.

"Sit down. No wonder you look ready to keel over." She shook her head and put her hand on Walker's forehead as if checking for a fever. She blushed and put her hand back down. She met Bram's eyes over Walker's head, thankful that her best friend hadn't growled for her being so close to another man during the mating heat. It was a testament to how strong Bram's will actually was that he could act so rational all the time. "I'm not a Healer, so I can't do anything for you other than tell you to sleep after you eat. You've taken all your energy stores, haven't you?" Healers only had so much energy within them to Heal their Pack. Yes, they could draw on the Alpha and the rest of the Pack in the process, but it still tired them out, and if they weren't careful, they could kill themselves. And she could have kissed the man after she kicked him for doing so much for Shane, and hurting himself in the process.

Walker closed his eyes, his face weary. "He needs to be fully healthy to make it tomorrow, and we both know that." That was all he said in answer. He didn't need to say anything else, as they all knew what was at stake at the next full moon.

"You need to go home and sleep," Bram said after a moment. "The hunt is tomorrow, and they'll need you." He paused. "We'll need you."

She and Bram would be hunting with the Talons the next night to be by Shane's side. It wasn't unheard of for the two Packs to share full moon hunts, but this one was special.

"I'll take him home." Brandon moved forward and pulled his brother, his fellow triplet, to his feet. "Come on, brother mine. I'll make you a nice steak and tuck you in with your blankie."

"I'd flip you off, but damn if that doesn't sound amazing."

Charlotte smiled at the two as they walked out of Shane's home despite the brevity of the situation. "Walker will be okay. I don't think the Brentwoods will let one of their own be in pain alone."

"Then we'd better make sure we Redwoods don't let Shane be alone right now. He's probably going to be sore since Walker's healing doesn't fix everything." Bram put his hand on the small of her lower back, and she sucked in a breath.

He'd always been so careful not to touch her.

She turned in his arms and cupped his face, knowing she was about to take a step that would once again change everything. "Thank you for saving him," she whispered. "And thank you for not getting hurt yourself." She brushed her lips across his, once, twice.

He stood still, his body hard against hers for a moment before pulling her closer with his hand on her back. His mouth parted and his tongue slid along her lips. She opened for him, savoring his taste, the feel of him, everything about him.

She pulled back before she could want too much, and far too quickly for either of them by the look in Bram's eyes.

"Let's go check on him."

He licked his lips, his eyes dark but for the bright yellow rim around the irises. "We're doing this," he growled softly. "When he's whole, when he's healthy, we're doing this."

There was no question about what *this* was, but she wasn't sure she was ready for that. A kiss was far from a declaration. An acceptance of fate. And a lifetime of heartache if the bond were to fail once more.

"I need more time."

He tilted his head. Oh, his wolf was close to the surface. So close.

"Then you'll have it. You need only ask, but I'm not giving up easily." He smiled then, a flash of teeth against dark skin that made her shiver. She loved it when he smiled, but he didn't do it often. "Now let's go see our boy."

Ours.

She liked the sound of that, even if she didn't know what to make of it. He slid his hand over hers, and they made their way into Shane's bedroom. The other part of their triad lay on his bed, his back propped up against pillows and a blanket covering most of his lower half. She'd known they'd stripped his bloody clothes from him, but she wasn't sure if he'd put anything else on after that. Just the thought that he could be naked under that very thin sheet sent shivers over her body.

Apparently, just the thought of both Bram and Shane could send her into chills and need.

"Walker going to be okay?" Shane asked. "He looked a little pale when he was leaving here."

Charlotte nodded and let go of Bram's hand to take a seat on the bed near Shane. Bram walked around to the other side and sat down, as well. The proximity of two very sexy men in bed with her did nothing to calm her wolf, but at this point, she figured she was beyond calming until the full moon.

Shane looked between the two of them, brows raised. "Something going on I should know about?"

With so much going on in her mind, and so many things that could go wrong, Charlotte did the only thing she could do. She leaned forward and cupped the side of Shane's face with her palm.

"They almost killed you." Her voice was a breathy whisper, but she was sure both men heard her.

Shane reached up and put his hand over hers. "They didn't."

"Gideon will take care of them." Bram's words made her turn toward them. "I don't know if they'll lose their lives, but I have a feeling a Pack meeting is on the way."

Shane frowned, and Charlotte wanted to kiss the look away. "I don't know how I feel about that."

Bram shrugged. "They went against their Alpha and tried to kill one of their own. Not sure if I feel much pity for them."

Charlotte blew out a breath. "The meeting, if it takes place at all, will happen after the hunt. It's too close to the full moon for that kind of tension out in the open like that." She rubbed her fingers along

Shane's temple, and he turned to look at her again. "I'm glad you're okay, and tomorrow, we'll run on four paws by your side." She blinked away tears, annoyed that she was letting her emotions get the best of her. "Don't do that again, okay? I don't think I can take it."

"I'll try not to." Shane's voice was a rough chuckle.

She leaned down then, brushing her lips along his, much as she'd done to Bram. But unlike with her best friend and lover, this was the first time she was tasting Shane. He tasted of sweetness and a little bit of rum. Walker must have given him a sip to help with the pain, as wolves couldn't have most medications. She deepened the kiss, needing to know for sure this man could be hers.

Her wolf howled, a celebration mixed with mourning. Once they made love, if the bond didn't take as it had before, her wolf would mourn for eternity.

Could Charlotte take that chance?

When Shane reached around to grip the back of her head, his fingers tangling in her hair, she knew she had to. There wasn't another choice.

Hiding from what they could be wouldn't help a single person. If she didn't take that leap, she'd hate herself until the end of her days.

She pulled away, her breathing heavy. "Wow."

Shane smiled then, his face going from merely handsome to stunning in the movement. "Glad to hear it."

"Do I get a turn?" Bram said from their side. She'd been aware he'd watched the entire time, and instead of feeling ashamed for kissing another man in front of him, she only got more turned on.

"I think that sounds like the best thing I've heard in a long while," Shane said, his voice full of laughter.

"Things sure do change daily around here, don't they?"

Charlotte laughed, pulling away a little more so Bram could move closer. "Well, we'll never be dull, that's for sure."

Bram leaned into Shane, his gaze intense. She sucked in a breath when Bram cupped the back of Shane's head and forced his mouth to his.

She'd known the two of them would scorch the earth, but she'd never known it would be like this.

It wasn't a truly hard kiss at first, a gentle crush that ascended into a powerful wave of emotion and passion. They kissed each other like they couldn't get enough of one another before breaking away, panting and filling her with need.

She licked her lips as the two men turned to face her.

"I think she liked it," Shane said softly.

"I know she did."

She rolled her eyes even as she laughed. "Well, yeah, hello. Of course, I did. You're both sex on a stick, and now you're touching and sweaty? Perfection."

"No, what would be perfection is if you scooted over just a bit so it would be the three of us," Shane corrected.

Though her body yearned to do just that, she stood up from the bed on shaky legs.

"After." Shane's face went crestfallen. "After the full moon and you're healthy. Then...well, then we'll see what happens."

And though that was the best decision in the long run, she knew none of them were going to be able to sleep that night.

She'd tasted both of her men, had them in her arms if only for the moment. She just prayed that when the moon rose full and high in the sky, she'd find the strength to keep them.

Because her heart had betrayed her once already, and she'd be damned if she'd let it happen again.

CHAPTER TEN

Bram didn't have a good feeling about this. The moon shone high in the sky, bright and beckoning. It pulled at his wolf, his skin itchy, as if too small for his body. His bones ached deep down, ready to break and transform into his other counterpart. Wolves didn't have to hunt on the full moon, and most didn't do so in such large groups every month. However, sometimes the occasion called for it. Tonight, he wouldn't run on four paws with his Pack, but rather the Talons. And while other Redwoods had hunted with the other Pack in the past for fun or because they were on their way to mating, Bram had never had the opportunity.

He was the Alpha's guard, an enforcer. From the time he'd hit puberty, he'd known his role, and Kade had figured it out, as well. He'd been running with the Alpha ever since.

Tonight, he wouldn't be, and he honestly wasn't sure how he felt about that.

It was something he'd need to get over though because while his wolf needed this run, tonight wasn't about him. Shane needed Bram and Charlotte by his side during his first shift, and that meant Bram would put aside his own reservations and worries and help the other man.

Bram couldn't remember not shifting into his wolf. He didn't even remember his first shift. Some people swore they could, even though they'd been too young. For most of them, it was their first memory.

Bram could only remember being wolf, never fighting the change.

So he wasn't sure how much help he'd be tonight, but if Shane needed him, he'd be there. He could still remember the taste of the other man's tongue on his, the feel of Shane's lips, the scrape of stubble against skin. His wolf had bucked at the reins, needing more, but it hadn't been the time.

When—not if—Shane made the change to wolf, they would all have to be ready to face the next step. His wolf was oddly content at that thought, but once again, Bram pushed that away.

Strong arms wrapped around his middle as Charlotte pressed herself to Bram's back. This time, his wolf wasn't merely content, but *ravenous*.

He slid his hands over hers before turning around in her arms. "Are you ready for tonight?"

She sighed into his chest, his strong girl looking vulnerable like she never could around others. "Yes, though I wish I weren't so nervous."

Bram kissed the top of her head, aware they'd been touching more now than they had in previous months. The two of them had always been close, holding one another like this when they needed to because it had been safe. When things had gone astray, they'd resisted the urge to do what had come naturally for so long.

Now he had her in his arms again, but it wasn't the same as last time. Instead, this was comfort wrapped in promise and heat. He'd missed the feel of her against him more than he'd ever thought possible. It had taken a human entering their lives for them to see the truth behind what they had been missing.

A human who wouldn't be human after tonight.

Though Bram and Charlotte were standing in the middle of a field on the Talon Pack land, they were early enough that they were alone. Soon, the rest of the Talons would show up already in wolf form or to begin shifting. While nudity didn't usually bother people, teens in the middle of finding out whom they were, preferred to shift indoors, as did some wolves who took a while to change.

The shift itself was personal, their bodies becoming their most vulnerable selves before they went from one form to another. It was a private thing that they could sometimes do in front of others if the time was right. A full moon hunt was usually one of those times.

Shane would shift tonight near Charlotte and Bram, but Walker and Gideon would be close, as well. Bram hoped everything would work out so that none of them were needed, but nothing so far had worked out as he'd planned so he wasn't sure.

Bram's wolf pushed at him just a bit more, and he turned as Shane walked toward them. The Brentwoods around him dispersed to their own areas, though Gideon and Walker followed him.

Charlotte slid from Bram's grasp and moved toward the other man. Again, he didn't feel the jealousy he would and did with any other man. It just proved to him that his was more than multiple potential mates. This was a triad.

Something that had never once crossed his mind as a possibility before this.

"Ready to do this?" Charlotte asked, her voice serious but still soft.

Shane nodded, though Bram noticed the slight fear in his eyes. That actually made Bram feel a bit better, as anyone with a brain would be a little scared in this situation.

"As ready as I'll ever be." Shane rubbed his shoulder over his shirt and winced. "Hell, my skin feels like it's being rubbed raw."

Bram moved forward and frowned. "Take off your shirt. Your skin is ultra sensitive right now, and anything on it is just going to hurt."

"I take it you want me to remove my pants, as well," Shane said dryly.

"You're going to have to sooner or later," Charlotte said evenly. "Did the others teach you the etiquette that comes with shifting in public?"

Shane pulled his shirt up over his head, and Bram did his best not to stare. As they were literally talking about etiquette right then, he knew he should probably follow the rules.

"They told me," Shane finally answered. "But they won't tell me how much this is going to hurt."

Bram met Charlotte's eyes for a brief moment before turning back to Shane. "A lot."

The other man blew out a breath. "I figured."

"I'm here to help if needed," Walker put in. "But I'm also here for all my wolves, so don't need me."

Gideon looked over Bram's shoulder and cursed. "Hell. Don't need me either. There's a pup over there on their first hunt, and they're scared as hell."

Bram turned around, aware the Alpha could sense changes within the Pack bonds far before anyone could sense things in the air.

"We can handle this," Bram promised, praying he wasn't lying.

"I hope so," the Alpha mumbled. "You've got this, Shane. Just let your wolf come out, listen to it, and breathe through the pain. Those around you have done this countless times and will lead you through it. I need to go help the pup right now, but I can be here on a moment's notice."

Shane shook his head, his body tense. "Help the kid. I'm not alone."

Gideon nodded and then ran off to where the child was.

"Where's Brie?" Shane asked before groaning. The other man fell to his knees, and Charlotte let out a curse before going to him. Bram followed but stayed silent.

"Breathe through the pain. Let's take off your pants since the change is coming on quick. And as for Brie, morning sickness came at night this time, so she's at home resting. Wolves don't *need* to change on the full moon, and she's been shifting often enough for it not to be a problem."

Bram helped Shane take off his pants, ignoring the man's naked state. Shane was in a hell of a lot of pain, and this wasn't the time to think about other things.

Other wolves around them began shifting like normal, but Bram stayed in human form, aware that Shane might need him. When the other man fell to the ground full, a scream ripping through his throat, Bram knew something was wrong.

"He's not shifting," Walker whispered.

"I know." Bram's jaw tightened, but he didn't move forward to touch Shane in comfort. Any contact right now would be excruciating.

Shane's body was covered in sweat, tense and corded muscle sliding over his body but not fully shifting. When going wolf, bones usually broke, and tendons tore, but there was an eventual outcome to the pain.

Bram knew there wouldn't be this time.

Shane screamed again, tears leaking from his eyes, Bram cursed. His wolf clawed at him, needing to help. But Bram knew of only one way to help right, then and he wasn't sure it would work at all.

"What are we going to do?" Charlotte asked. She was on her knees by Shane's side, running her hands through his hair. It was probably the only part of him she could touch right now without making it worse.

Shane coughed, blood spattering over Charlotte's legs, and she looked up at Bram, fear in her eyes.

"Fuck." Bram went to his knees. "I don't think this is working."

Shane rolled over, his eyes wide as he looked at both of them. "It's like I'm being ripped apart, but can't do anything about it." He coughed again, spraying more blood on the ground.

Walker was on his knees beside Shane, as well. "We'd hoped having him near the Pack when he shifted the first time would help his wolf find his way, but now I'm thinking we should have had him in the infirmary."

Bram looked over his shoulder and studied the others. Most were shifting or had already shifted, preoccupied with their own moments. Only a few were looking over at them, worried looks on their faces. Gideon was still with the child, holding the little boy close to him as it panted hard. If Gideon left right now to help Shane, the pup could hurt himself, and no one wanted that.

"There's only one way," Bram growled out. He cupped Shane's face, ignoring the way the other man winced at the contact. "I think whatever the serum did to you, it wasn't enough. It only mimics certain parts of the shift, but doesn't give you everything you need to become one of us."

Walker checked Shane's pulse and cursed. "That's what I'm thinking now, too."

Shane gripped Bram's wrist. "Don't let me die in front of her," he whispered.

"I'm sitting right here, and you aren't going to die." Charlotte kissed Shane's forehead, and the other man cried out in pain. All of this contact on his skin had to be excruciating.

"Gideon is helping the pup, but I think someone needs to actually change you," Bram put in.

Shane's eyes widened. "Well hell."

"My sentiments exactly," Bram said dryly.

"Only an Alpha or a wolf *very* close to Alpha status can change a wolf," Walker said softly. "If Gideon is busy..."

"I can do it," Bram said matter-of-factly. "I...I can do it." He'd never changed a wolf before. Never had to. But he knew he could bring out the wolf within Shane. He'd hidden his strength for so long, others had forgotten how strong his wolf truly was. It wasn't that he'd been ashamed of it, but more that he hadn't known how to fit in. How to make things work within a Pack where wolves would constantly need to fight for dominance against him and lose. He wasn't as strong as Kade or Gideon, but he had a feeling, if needed, he could take out their Betas and Heirs.

He never would, though. That wasn't who he was. But now, if he needed to save Shane's life, he'd show the others who he truly was and do what he had to do.

Damn the consequences.

Walker let out a breath. "If you do this..."

"Let him," Shane bit out, his lips covered in blood. "I trust him."

Charlotte put Shane's head on her lap and whispered soothing words. "Shift into your wolf quickly, Bram. We don't have a lot of time."

Walker blew out a breath. "I knew you were stronger than you let on but are you sure?"

Bram met the other man's eyes. "I'm sure."

And with that, Bram quickly stripped and pulled on the cord that connected him with his wolf. His body twisted and turned, his bones breaking, moving into new positions. Normally, it would take him a good five minutes to complete the shift, but he didn't have that kind of time, and his wolf seemed to understand that.

Once wolf, he padded over to Shane and met the other man's gaze.

Shane smiled, though it was weak. "Never saw you in your wolf form. Kind of like it." Bram huffed and looked over at Charlotte. She pushed at Shane's shoulders, pinning down his arms, even as she nodded.

Walker held onto Shane's legs, and Bram leapt.

He didn't know why he knew this, but he *knew* he didn't need to bite him as hard or as much as he would have if Shane had been fully human. It was almost as if the moon goddess herself were speaking to him. He bit into Shane's side and then his thigh. Only two bites, but they would be enough.

He honestly didn't know *why* he understood that. It wasn't as if Bram ever truly gave in to fate, especially after what had happened with Charlotte the first time, but he couldn't help but give in now.

Shane thrashed but didn't scream. In fact, after the two bites when Bram moved back, Shane seemed to calm. He looked over at Bram, met his gaze, and blinked.

Bram wanted to shift back to speak but froze when Shane arched his back and let out a rough shout. Charlotte immediately moved back, as did Walker. The three of them watched as Shane slowly shifted from man to wolf.

While Bram was a dark black wolf, and Charlotte was a slightly lighter one with touches of red in her fur, Shane proved to be a milk chocolate brown. His fur was sweat-slick, and his eyes huge with fear, but he was *whole.*

"Oh, thank the goddess," Charlotte whispered. She crawled forward, her hands out to him. "Shane, it's me. Are you okay?"

Shane stared at her for a moment before trying to nod. Only in wolf form, it wasn't so easy so he looked a bit awkward. It didn't matter though. Shane was alive. He was wolf. And from the look in Walker's eyes, he was still Pack.

Things had changed once again, but Bram would never regret what he'd had to do.

Shane was wolf.

Finally.

****

Shane felt as if he were a baby giraffe learning to walk for the first time. His legs weren't moving the way they should, and he kept falling flat on his face. He couldn't quite put into words the amount of pain he'd been in before, but right then, he knew that whatever had been done had been for *this.*

He was a wolf. A freaking *shifter.* And now that he was in this form, he could sense the bonds the others had mentioned. Before it had been like there was a film over them, hiding them, stopping them from being what he thought they should be. But now he was slowly waking up from the murkiness.

Hell, he could even sense Charlotte and Bram more now than he had before. And if he was feeling what they were feeling, he had no idea how they could have held themselves back from him and each other for as long as they had.

They held a true strength. One that he might one day learn himself.

Bram was already shifted, and Charlotte had moved off to the side to do her shift, as well. He was happy with that because he wasn't sure he could handle her nakedness right now, or allow anyone else to see her either. He didn't know where all this possessiveness came from, but he had a feeling if he didn't rein it in, Charlotte would kick his ass. She was no weak wolf.

While Shane tried to get his bearings, his body still weak and his senses on overload, Gideon jogged toward them.

"You bit him?" he asked Bram, who had shifted back to human. Shane knew it took a tremendous amount of energy to do two full shifts back-to-back as Bram had done, and he had no idea how Bram was still awake, let alone standing guard over Charlotte as she shifted.

"It was the only way." The words came out as a rough growl, and Shane frowned. He slowly toddled his way over to Bram's side, leaning his new body along Bram's legs.

Bram looked down, his brows high, and ran a hand over Shane's head. The feeling of Bram's fingers through his fur was intoxicating. He leaned harder but moved his gaze toward Gideon. He didn't know if Bram was supposed to do what he'd done, and from the way Walker had freaked, it had been unusual for sure. Bram had saved his life, though, and he was Shane's mate, something he was still getting used to. He didn't want Bram to be in trouble for what had happened.

Gideon held up his hands. "I'm glad you were able to do it. Our Packs are changing, Bram. There are stronger wolves out there now than there were before. Kade and I knew that and have been prepared for this. I don't think anyone is at your level yet where they can change other wolves, but they could be soon. And when that happens, our laws will have to evolve much like you guys are. It's okay. I promise. Kade and I knew you were stronger than you let on. Just breathe."

Bram seemed to relax, and Shane tried to catch the undercurrents of the conversation but failed. It was all a little too much on his system right then.

Gideon looked down at Shane. "You're still Talon, and one hell of a big wolf. Welcome to the Pack." He grinned then, and Shane met the other man's eyes before lowering them. His wolf didn't want to antagonize, and Shane knew he'd have to learn more about this new version of himself day by day.

"I didn't know if Bram biting you would bring you into the Redwoods or not, but I had a feeling you'd stay Talon. You were brought in differently than any other member here, and I have a feeling no matter what happens, you'll always be Talon."

Shane tilted his head.

"That means when the mating bond takes place, and the Alphas are ready, Charlotte and I will be Talons, not Redwoods anymore," Bram explained. "But that's something we can talk about later. For now, just get used to your new wolf, okay?"

Hell. Apparently, the way he'd become a wolf was going to screw everyone over. Gideon didn't seem worried about it, but he had a feeling the Alpha was well trained in hiding what he was thinking. There were things going on around him that he didn't understand, but Shane knew he'd have to figure it out soon.

Gideon knelt down so he was at eye-level with Shane. "I need you to shift back soon. You're too new as a wolf to stay in this form for long. And because most wolves don't change immediately after a bite like that, you're still on a different path than the others. I don't want you to tire yourself out to the point of pain because you're so immersed in your new self. So change back. I know Charlotte needs to run and will do so, but then the three of you can rest."

"I'll make sure he's safe," Bram said. "I'll lead him through the change if you need to go."

Gideon raised a brow as he stood. "I see." The Alpha studied Bram, and Shane wasn't sure he liked it. "If you become Talon, you might be my lieutenant from the strength of your wolf. Are you ready for something like that."

Bram raised his chin. "We'll cross that bridge when we get to it."

"Sounds like a plan. Call me if you need me, but I have a feeling Shane will be just fine." He looked down and smiled. "Isn't that right, soldier?" And with that, Gideon trotted off toward another grouping of wolves that needed their Alpha.

Before Shane could try and figure out how to communicate, Charlotte moved toward them. While she was gorgeous in her human form, her wolf form was just as stunning. Shane wanted to rub against her and mark her as his, but he had a feeling tonight wasn't the night to do that.

Bram smiled at her, his grin wide, and Shane almost took a step back at the sheer emotion on his face. It was true that these two had known each other far longer than Shane, but one day, he hoped he could find that connection, as well.

He honestly didn't know how he'd ended up thinking about a future with the two of them, but now that he had, he knew he just needed to dive in full force. There was no use looking back and being fearful when others were counting on you.

"I'll stay here while he shifts back if you want to go for a run."

Charlotte gave a slight nod before walking up to Shane's side. She slid her body against his before nipping at his ear. Before he could figure out how to respond, she rubbed along Bram's legs and licked his fingers when he reached out to pet her.

Then she ran off, and Shane was left staring at her as she disappeared.

Bram let out a rough chuckle. "She has a way of doing that." They both stared after her for a bit longer before Bram finally moved. "Let's get you back to your human form while we wait for her. It's been a long night."

Shane wasn't sure he was in the mood to go through all that pain again to shift back, but he was in no shape to argue.

"I want you to look deep inside and try to find the piece of yourself connected to your wolf. Once you find that cord, pull on it. Imagine yourself as human, and let the change come over you. Don't fight it."

Shane wasn't sure he understood Bram's words, but he followed his instructions anyway. After all, Bram had saved his life more than once, and Shane would do anything to repay him. Even something as simple as just listening.

The cord connecting him to his wolf was a dark strand he'd never seen before, never felt before. He tugged on it, and the primal part of him that made him want to growl and bite tugged back. Shane wasn't sure what to do next, but Bram put his hand on Shane's back.

"I want to talk to the man who will be my mate. Let that happen."

With that idea in his mind, his wolf changed course. They both wanted to talk to Bram apparently. He pictured himself as human, and let out a howl as his body began to shift back.

Sweaty, sore, and exhausted, Shane lay in the grass, naked as the day he was born. Bram laughed when as he sat next to him, equally naked.

"You look ready to nap, but I figured you'd probably want to sleep at home."

Shane rolled over and leaned on his arm. "Charlotte should be back soon, right?"

Bram nodded. "And I think the two of us will stay with you tonight, if that's okay?"

The look in the other man's eyes made Shane's dick harden, and he swallowed, though his mouth was dry.

Before Shane could think of what to say, Charlotte trotted up. She looked between the two of them, her eyes filled with knowing, and moved to a grouping of bushes to shift back.

Shane wasn't sure what would happen once they got back to his place, but he knew that everything would be different afterward. His wolf wanted them, and he had a feeling his human half wanted them even more.

He'd never thought to find someone—or more than one someone—to be with for the long haul, but he wasn't human any longer. Whatever was inside him, this new soul, this new wolf, wanted these two. And now he *knew* that whatever danger he faced, whatever war came at them, he would be stronger, *they* would be stronger as one.

He stood on shaky legs as Charlotte came out of the bushes, her simple dress covering her curves. He would strip that off her later, he knew.

"Are you ready to go home?" he asked, his voice like gravel.

Charlotte stood right in front of him and cupped his face. "I'm ready."

He wrapped his arm around her waist and tugged her close before crushing his mouth to hers. She tasted of power and sweetness, and he wanted her mouth all over him.

When he pulled away, Bram was there, kissing him even harder. Shane finally caught a breath when Bram and Charlotte kissed each other, but the sight didn't stop the rapid beat of his heart.

They were going to do this.

He was wolf. He was Talon.

And soon...soon, he'd have mates.

A far cry from the human soldier he'd been before all of this, but he knew this was where he was supposed to be. Where he was meant to be all along.

Finally.

BRANDON

Brandon fell to his knees, his body shaking. He hadn't gone on the hunt tonight for this very reason, and yet it seemed he still hadn't been able to fully cope with the ever-changing bonds of his Pack.

He was the Omega. The one wolf who should be able to handle the emotions and tensions of a Pack of shifters. A Pack that had gone through hell but had clawed its way back to health and life.

Yet he couldn't do it.

His body shuddered, and he emptied the contents of his stomach on his hardwood floor. Sweat covered his body, and he knew he was too weak to shift into wolf form at the moment. His Pack needed him to be healthy. To be whole.

But he wasn't.

And now there was a new member of his Pack, a new bond that was different than the others. But for some reason, Brandon didn't think this bond would break them. No, the new wolf, this former human who had sacrificed everything for them, could be the one thing that could protect them.

Brandon just had to pray he would live long enough to see it.

His wolf needed a mate.

His darkness needed a light.

And with each passing day, each new emotion that tugged at his soul, each new worry and fear over a war they might not win, he knew his battle might be lost.

Shane might be able to save the Pack's future, but Brandon wasn't sure anything would be strong enough to save him.

Things were changing, and Brandon couldn't keep up.

And a Pack without an Omega wasn't a Pack that could survive.

I need a mate, he said to himself once again.

Only he wasn't sure he knew where to look.

CHAPTER ELEVEN

Charlotte's heart was going to beat straight out of her chest. She'd run as wolf alongside others of her kind, her four paws pounding the ground. Those she'd run with hadn't been Pack, but if she followed the path laid in front of her, they soon would be.

Outside the four walls of Shane's home, a war was brewing. Humans knew of the wolves' existence. Some wanted their heads, others to study what made wolves bleed. Some were fascinated by shifters, fanatics dangerously obsessed, forming passels of groupies and fans that Charlotte would never understand. None of the Packs ignored them, but those who begged to be changed or wanted a shifter in their bed weren't what her people were concentrating on at the moment. No, they were more focused on their own government. The same government that was divided about what to do with the "shifter problem." Some wanted to tag and collar them. Others wanted to study them.

Senators like McMaster wanted to call them animals, strip away their rights and privileges as humans and citizens.

Men like Montag took their greed and cruelty to the next level and created life and death in their labs.

The war was brewing. The battles outside their doors escalating.

But right now, this wasn't about that.

This was about the three people, the three wolves, in this room, and what they were about to do. There was no fighting the attraction any longer. No begging for the pull to dissipate.

They would make love as one and bite into each other's shoulders to form mating marks.

And if the moon goddess shined on them, they would create a mating bond.

It was a little too much for Charlotte to absorb...so she didn't try.

Tonight, she would just *feel*.

Tomorrow she could worry.

And pray for more tomorrows.

Shane cupped her face, and she looked up at him. "You're in your head again," he murmured. "What are you thinking about?"

She leaned into his hand, enjoying the way his eyes darkened. "About everything."

"That's a lot to have on your mind," Bram said from behind her. He put his hands on her hips, and she sucked in a breath. Both men were so much larger than she was, so freaking big height and width-wise with their breadth of muscle. Yet she knew they would never hurt her.

Perhaps not physically, she thought.

But emotionally? She couldn't help but be fearful of that break she'd endured with Bram.

Not again.

She would not break again.

"I was actually trying to get everything out of my mind."

"Everything?" Shane teased, his thumb brushing along her cheek.

She wrapped her arms around his waist, pulling him close. His rock-hard erection pressed firmly against her belly as Bram's did the same to her lower back.

"Not everything," she breathed. "Not everything."

"I never knew I could want someone this much," Shane said softly, his lips a bare inch from hers. "How can I want you, want Bram, as much as I do, and yet know nothing about you?"

"You know the important things," she said as she arched her neck for Bram's lips. She shivered in their hold. She'd had her best friend's lips on her before, but it had been nothing like this. Their mating before had been happiness, friendship, and promise. Now...there was trepidation that mixed with the heat and chemistry that came with not one, but two men who wanted her.

Who needed her.

Who she, in turn, craved, as well.

"You'll know more after tonight, and more in the days to come," she added. Her hands slid up Shane's back, his body sweat-slick from the change, but hard, ready.

"You have the softest skin," Shane murmured. "Doesn't she, Bram?"

Bram's hand slid up underneath the bottom of her tank to cup her breast. His thumb brushed her nipple and her inner walls clenched, wet, *ready*...for them both. He rocked into her, and she arched for him. The action pushed her breasts into Shane's chest as well as Bram's hand.

She kept her eyes open, watching the way Shane's darkened and that little ring of yellow around his eyes began to glow. That came with either intense arousal or his wolf coming to the surface. Right then, she had a feeling it was a little bit of both. With any other wolf, in any other way of creating a new shifter, what Shane was doing right now wouldn't have been possible. He shouldn't have been able to shift so soon after a bite, shouldn't have been able to feel the intense pull towards her and Bram as he was. He also shouldn't have the control he did to hold her so close and not pound her against a wall with such intensity that they'd be a pile of limbs in the end.

That would come soon, she knew, but Shane was like no other wolf.

And he'd been practicing his control with her and Bram for enough time that she knew whatever happened tonight, it would be *him*, and not his lack of control.

"She's soft everywhere, Shane," Bram finally answered, pulling Charlotte into the present. She hadn't been too far gone, though, not with both of them touching her as they were. "Wait until you taste her. Like sugar and silk."

With one hand on her breast, Bram slid the other under the top of her leggings to cup her. She moaned, unable to hold the sound back. She hadn't worn panties or a bra to shift as it would have only gotten in the way, and now she had a feeling all three of them would enjoy the lack of barriers. And the men wore only sweats—no underwear, no shirts.

Just hard men, hard cocks, and a need for her.

Her body melted into them both. She hadn't thought it would be so hot to have two men touch her, hold her, *need* her, and at the same time, talk about her with her in the room as if they couldn't get enough of her.

Despite her past and what she'd thought her entire life, Charlotte was indeed a lucky woman tonight.

And perhaps for longer than a single night if things worked out the way they should. The way they could.

Shane kissed her then, his tongue sliding along hers in a sexual caress that made her want to wrap her leg around his waist and rock against him until she came. Seeming to know that, Bram slid his fingers over her clit, finding her wet and ready for them. He groaned into her shoulder, sliding two fingers deep inside. At the feeling of his fingers so deep inside her cunt, she gasped into Shane's mouth. He took the sound and deepened the kiss, wrapping his arms around her and Bram. When Bram groaned behind her, she had a feeling Shane was holding their other man and not her.

Goddess, how had this happened? How had she gone from a broken wolf to a woman with not one, but two men? She didn't deserve this, but she was just selfish enough to take it and never let go.

She pulled away, gasping. "Tonight, if the moon goddess shines her light on us, there will be a bond. Are you okay with that?" She wasn't sure if she was asking Bram or Shane, or even herself at that moment.

Shane kissed her chin then moved over her head to do the same to Bram.

Seriously, freaking hot as hell.

"I don't know about the moon goddess, but what I'm feeling isn't going away. It hasn't since I first saw you. And yeah, it's taking a leap of faith, but I know deep down in my gut that this is the right thing to do.

We're stronger together than we are apart, and I know I don't want to face what's to come without you. Without either of you."

Charlotte turned then, forcing Bram's hold on her to lessen. He slid his hands over her hips instead, and she rested her back on Shane's front. "And you?"

Bram frowned, and her heart ached. What if he said no? What if he walked away because she hadn't been enough the first time?

When he let out a low growl, this one far more dangerous than anything let out during heat, her eyes widened.

"If I see you giving me that look again, I'm going to bend you over my knee and spank you." His voice was low, deadly.

"I might like to see that," Shane said with a teasing tone to his voice. "Just saying."

Bram snapped his teeth at Shane but winked. Then he looked down at her and glowered. "You are my mate. You were before, and you are now. We didn't bond before because we didn't have Shane. It's as simple as that. And if you keep looking at me like you think you aren't good enough because of where you came from, I'm going to be fucking angry. You get me? So stop doing this bullshit, and let me fucking kiss you. Then let me fuck you. And then let me bite you." He paused. "You know what, fuck that. I'm going to kiss you. Then I'm going to fuck you. Then I'm going to bite you. You don't need to *let* me because I'm going to take it. I'm done waiting for you, being the patient best friend who had to watch you die a little more inside until Shane showed up. I'm taking what's mine. Taking you." He looked over her head. "And I'm taking Shane."

She swallowed hard, her body so rigid she could barely breathe. She didn't know what to say, so she just said what was on her mind. "I think I almost came from those words alone. So, yeah, take me. Take *us*. I'm ready, and you're not going to find anyone unwilling here."

Shane cleared his throat. "Well if I had any reservations before this, they are sure as hell gone now. Fuck, Bram. You need to speak like that all the time." He stopped, and she looked up at him over her shoulder. "Wait, not all the time. Just with me and Charlotte because I sure as hell don't want anyone else hearing that. It's just for us."

Charlotte smiled then, a smile she hadn't given anyone in a long time. "Just for us."

Bram licked his lips, a wicked gleam in his eyes. "Good." He looked up at Shane. "You know how mating works, right?"

Charlotte turned in their arms so she could see them both. Their hands were still all over each other, but now she didn't have to crane her neck.

"You explained about sex and the mating mark. But with three people, I'm not sure how that will work."

"There needs to be...penetration with all of us somehow," Bram continued, and Charlotte rolled her eyes. This was not the time to be scared of the big words. And the fact that she was the one thinking that just told her how on edge these two made her.

"Both of you will need to come inside me," she explained. "Maybe not at the same time since I'm not sure I'm exactly ready for that."

Shane's eyes widened. "So later, then?"

She let out a breath. "What is it with guys and anal?"

Bram chuckled. "Well, as I'm going to also fuck Shane, I'd say we like anal just fine."

Shane barked out a laugh. "Oh yeah? What if I want to be the one that fucks you?"

Yep, Charlotte was going to pass out from pleasure tonight. She was sure of it.

"We'll take turns," Bram said with a grin. "If you can take me that is."

Charlotte's knees gave out, and Bram quickly swept her into his arms. "Did I just swoon?"

Shane looked down at her, a wide and cocky grin on his face. "Hell yeah, you did. I do believe our little wolf likes the idea of you and me tangling, Bram. What do you think?"

Bram led her to the bedroom with Shane at his side. "I think we are two lucky ass wolves. And as for the mating bond, as long as the three of us somehow all make it work, the bond should form. I know I sound clinical right now, but bear with me. The only other triad I know has a wolf, a witch, and a partial demon. Not three wolves, one of which was formed just a little differently."

Charlotte wiggled, and Bram set her down on her feet at the foot of the bed. "You talked to my aunt and uncles?" She didn't know why, but after all of that, she finally blushed.

Bram shrugged. "I wanted to make sure we didn't miss anything this time. I'll be damned if the bond doesn't take because we missed something."

"So you're saying we need to try *all* the positions," Shane said with a laugh. "Well, it's a good thing Walker mentioned a shifter's stamina then."

Both Charlotte and Bram growled, and Shane held up his hands. "What?"

"Why were you talking to Walker about sex?" Bram asked.

"I asked what other things came with being a wolf. *He* was being clinical. Not you. Just breathe, okay? You're the only two for me."

Charlotte relaxed, surprised at the jealousy that had coursed through her.

Bram's body also lost some of its tension behind her. "Good. Now that we've talked this to death, how about we get back to where we started? Because it's going to be a fantastically long night, and I can't wait to have you."

Though her body had cooled somewhat when they'd been talking, the look in Bram's eyes brought her right back.

"Just make love to me," she said finally. "We'll make it work."

They had to.

The men shared a look, then they *moved*.

Bram was at her front, cupping her face with his hands and kissing her like there was no tomorrow. She breathed in the scent of him, her wolf pushing at her, needing her mates. Shane was at her back and slowly slid his hands down her sides to cup her ass before kneeling behind her. She gasped as he pulled her leggings down in one movement. When he tugged, she helped him take them fully off and could barely think before Bram pulled her top over her head. That left her naked in front of her two men, and with the looks they were giving her, she knew she'd never felt as cherished and sexy as she did right then.

Shane went back to his knees and started massaging her butt, leaving trails of kisses before spreading her and licking up her cunt. She bent forward slightly, her body humming as he flicked his tongue over her clit before feasting. Bram had moved to cup her breasts, taking one nipple in his mouth and using his fingers to pluck at the other one.

There were so many hands, so much sensation; she couldn't focus on both of them.

And when Bram slid his hand down her stomach and to her clit to play alongside Shane's tongue, she came.

"Hell," Shane bit out as he stood up again. "You are fucking gorgeous when you come, baby."

She blinked up at him before smiling wide. "I'm glad you think so." And with that, she went down to her knees. Before either man could say anything, she had their pants lowered and a cock in each hand. She pumped them once before licking the crown of Bram's and then doing the same to Shane's.

She was a dominant female wolf.

One of the fastest wolves within these two Packs.

And yet right then, she knew she'd never felt this bold, this fierce, this *feminine* before.

She wanted to take them both in her mouth, but her men had other ideas. *Her men.* She could get used to the sound of that.

Shane had her on her back on the bed and his mouth between her legs once again. Bram had kicked off his sweats, as had Shane apparently, and was behind Shane, doing something to the other man to make him moan.

"Get in me," she cried out as Shane made her come. Again. "I'm not going to last the night if you guys keep making me come without your cocks in me."

Shane snorted. "Well, if you're going to be like that." His eyes crossed, and he leaned over her. She took that as a good excuse to kiss his jaw and run her hands over his chest.

"What's Bram doing back there?" she teased.

Bram moved to the side of Shane and licked his lips. "Just making sure our soldier here is ready." He waved a bottle of lube, and she blinked.

"Where did you get that? I didn't see you move."

Bram shrugged. "I might have left a bag underneath Shane's bed just in case."

"Got to like a man who's prepared...holy mother of God," Shane breathed. "Right there, Bram. Holy...okay, I need to get in you Charlotte, or I'm going to come like a teenager right now all over your stomach, and I'd rather feel your sweet heat around me."

She put her hands on his cheeks and brought him in for a kiss. "Then fuck me, Shane. Show me I'm yours."

Shane bit down on her lower lip. "As long as you do the same for me."

"Deal," she breathed.

He positioned himself at her entrance and then slowly filled her. Her breath quickened, and she arched her back, taking him in deeper.

"Keep going," Bram ordered from behind Shane. Charlotte looked up to see Bram's hands on Shane's hips, moving the man so the three of them were connected. "Make her ours, Shane, and when you're fully seated, I'm going to do the same for you. You ready for that? I'm going to have my cock deep in your ass. You've only had my fingers tonight, but you're ready for me aren't you?"

Sweat slid down Shane's chest, and Charlotte could barely breathe. She honestly couldn't comprehend everything right now. It was too much, everything was too much, and yet she never wanted it to end.

When Shane fully entered her, she wrapped one leg tightly around his waist and used the other to bring Bram closer.

"Now," Shane barked. "Fuck me now, Bram, then we'll make love to our Charlotte, our mate."

Mate.

Goddess how she'd wanted to hear that word. Always. And now she would have *two*.

The bond *had* to work. There was no other option, not anymore. Not when she'd lost her heart not only to Bram, but now Shane, as well. The man who had sacrificed everything for people he didn't know and a cause he found just.

Bram moved, and Shane's breath went choppy. Soon, Bram was so close to Shane's back she knew he'd entered the other man, hot, ready, *needy*.

"Move," she panted. "Please. I'm so close. *Move*."

And they did. As one, Bram and Shane somehow found a rhythm where Bram made love to Shane, Shane to Charlotte, and when Charlotte arched her hips to meet them, she made love to both of them.

It was beautiful, everything it should have been with just Bram, but more than it could have been at any other time.

Her wolf paced, ready for the mating mark. As her body heated, her nipples hardening to the point where it hurt, she crashed over the edge of pleasure and came. Shane followed, Bram's and Charlotte's names on his lips, and when Bram shouted, she knew he'd come, as well.

And just like that, the first spark of the bond snapped into place. She could *feel* Shane deep inside her, not just her body, but in her heart, her soul.

Her wolf cried out in joy, and tears slid down Charlotte's cheeks.

Her fangs elongated, and she bit into Shane's shoulder, marking him as hers. When she released him, she panted as Shane did the same to her. They hadn't had to teach him how to claim another. It was as instinctual as shifting, as being wolf. Bram had also bitten Shane's other shoulder, cementing the men together.

"Mate," she whispered, cupping Shane's face.

"Mine," he whispered and kissed her. "I can feel you and Bram. *Both* of you."

She smiled. The bond had worked for Bram and Shane, as well as her and Shane. Now she needed her Bram, her other mate, the other part of her soul, the other part of her future.

Bram slowly moved away, his eyes wide and glassy, but she knew it was the pure emotion, the same as she felt. They hadn't had a plan as to who would mate first, who would have their human halves mate first before marking them as wolves.

"I need you, too," she said softly as Shane pulled out of her, moving out of the way so Bram could come to her.

"Then take me," Bram said simply. Only it wasn't so simple. It never was.

She wasn't sure what she would do next, but Shane took the choice from her. He lifted her up from the bed and put her in Bram's arms. He got up from the bed quickly and came back with a couple of warm cloths. He wiped Bram's cock down before doing the same to her with the other one. She blinked as Bram sat down at the edge of the bed with Shane sidling up right behind him. She had a feeling the other man was exhausted after everything that had come that day and just needed to be near them as she and Bram completed their part of the bond.

Shane wrapped his arms around Bram's middle and bit into his shoulder. At the same time, Charlotte slid herself over Bram's already hard cock. All three of them moaned, even if Shane's was a bit muffled.

She would never get enough of this. Never get enough of them. Somehow, despite it all, she'd found the two men who could complete who she thought she'd never be.

They made her whole.

They made her strong.

They made her...theirs.

Charlotte put one hand on Shane's shoulder, the other on Bram, and rocked herself along Bram's lap.

Bram narrowed his eyes, then, his wolf at the surface. He lifted her up ever so slightly, to ram up into her. She called out but didn't have time to catch her breath as he continued to fuck her. Shane played with her nipples as well as Bram's, and she couldn't hold back any longer.

She came, bringing Bram with her. She couldn't breathe, couldn't think.

Their bond snapped into place, as well, a lock of pulsing sensation that connected the three of them in a way she hadn't thought possible.

Bram bit into her shoulder, marking her as his, and her wolf howled in pure pleasure. When her new mate turned his head to the side, she bit him, as well, leaving a mating mark that would tell everyone around them that he was *hers*. Shane was *hers,* as well.

And when the final part of the mating bond was complete, she burst into tears.

She could feel her men, feel her mates. They were everything she thought she couldn't have, everything she never knew she wanted. For a moment, she could only think of the pain that had come when the bond hadn't shown up the first time.

She hated crying and didn't do it often. But now she couldn't stop. It was just too much. She felt *everything,* and it warred within her. Somehow, she found herself lying in bed, sandwiched between her two men.

They held her close but didn't say anything. They didn't need to. They all felt what the others were feeling.

She knew this intensity would fade soon, but for now, she could ignore the world. Ignore the problems that would arise in the morning. Now, she could focus on her mates, her life, and the fact that she was warm for the first time in far too long.

She wasn't the same Charlotte who had been chained in the basement any longer.

She was stronger.

She was fiercer.

And she wasn't alone.

Now she just had to figure out what to do about it.

CHAPTER TWELVE

They weren't Talons yet, but Bram knew it was only a matter of time. And because of that, he would listen to what Gideon had to say and take each word in measure.

It had only been a day since Bram had created a mating bond with both Shane and Charlotte, but they were already doing their best to find a way to make things work.

Bram had honestly thought they'd wake up in the morning and find themselves Talons, or perhaps even find Shane a Redwood. But that hadn't happened. Instead, Shane remained a Talon Pack member, while Bram and Charlotte were still Redwoods. It wasn't exactly how things went for most of the other wolves that mated across Pack lines, but their triad mating was anything but usual.

Soon they'd have to make a choice, but he had a feeling they would end up Talons anyway. Gideon was *sure* that Shane could never break from the Talons now, and had said as much when they'd shown up at the Alpha's house that morning. And because Bram trusted Gideon, almost as much as he trusted his own

Alpha, he knew soon he and Charlotte would have to take that plunge.

In all honesty, it wasn't a choice at all, and that was something he'd have to get used to.

Everything was far messier, far more out of sync than most matings. "Anything worth doing is hard," his mother had used to say when he was a pup. And though he could barely remember the sound of her voice, he could still hear those words.

He pushed away the sadness that came with thinking of his mother and father, and focused on the Talon Alpha in front of him. His parents were long gone, and he'd mourned for them. Now it was time for him to find his new path with two wolves he'd never seen coming.

Charlotte was out on patrol with the Talons, not the Redwoods. Kade had thought it would be a good idea for her to learn to work with the new wolves. Bram had never been prouder. She was such a fast wolf, such a fantastic dominant female, but it was hard for her to look beyond her past to see that. It wasn't his role to show her how brilliant she was, however. That had to be all her. He could nudge her a bit, of course, and he had been trying to do that for years.

Hopefully, a new Pack who hadn't seen her as she was as a child would help. While the Redwoods had never treated her differently, she had felt it anyway because of the pressure she put on herself.

Now, Bram and Shane stood with Gideon in his home to talk about what would come next. It was all a little surreal, but he wouldn't be who he was if he couldn't roll with the punches.

"We still have the three wolves who attacked you in custody," Gideon was saying. "Kameron has his people on guard." Gideon frowned. "I know others want me to call a Pack circle to decide what to do, but I don't think that would be good for the Pack moral. However, these wolves betrayed us, betrayed you. So I'm going to take your input into consideration, Shane."

Bram's eyes widened. While Kade listened to his wolves, for some reason, Bram had always thought Gideon was a little more of a dictator than his Alpha. It seemed Bram had been wrong, and for that, he was very thankful.

Shane ran a hand over his face, and Bram put his hand on the other man's knee. Gideon didn't look surprised at the display of affection. The other man would clearly be able to see the mating marks at the collars of their shirts, scent them all over each other, and feel the bond between them. Bram knew all three of them—him, Shane, and Charlotte—were so blatantly into each other that even the weakest wolf would be able to tell at the moment.

"I don't know the options here," Shane said bluntly. "I think everyone is forgetting that I was a human man in the military less than a month ago."

Hell, had it only been that long? That was crazy.

"Fair enough," Gideon said after a moment. "For what they've done, they could be put to death. We can shun then from the Pack, break the bonds that make them Talon. We could lower their ranking within the Pack itself and force them to work up through the system over time like they did their entire adult lives. There are a few other options, but those are the main three." Gideon paused. "The main three that I'm willing to do right now."

Bram breathed in through his nose, letting the scent of Alpha and Shane roll over him. This would be Shane's and Gideon's decision, but Bram would be here no matter what happened.

"They thought I was the enemy when they came after me," Shane began. "They didn't know the truth, and while they should have trusted you and your word, they were scared. So, yeah, they need to learn the chain of command and maintain that, but killing them or pushing them out into the world without a bond during the unrest we have outside the wards right now seems cruel."

Gideon's shoulders relaxed marginally. If Bram hadn't been watching the other man, he would have missed it. It seemed Shane had passed some sort of test, or rather; the Alpha was pleased with Shane's words.

"You're thinking the same as I am, then," Gideon said, confirming Bram's thoughts. "Pull their ranks and make them work for it."

"I also want to show them that I'm not the enemy," Shane said earnestly. "I want to show all of you. I need to pull my weight."

Gideon studied the other man. "You will. You already have with what you've given us. We're still waiting on retaliation and what McMaster might do on the other end, but for now, we're training and keeping our people safe."

"It's not enough, though. I need to feel like I have a purpose."

"Then train with Bram, train with the Talons. And let's see what your wolf can do. Once we figure that out, we can see where you fit, and what role you'll play in the grander scheme of things. Breathe, Shane. You've been wolf for all but a day, and you have two new mates that need to know you, as well. We'll be here when you're on your feet. Now, go take time to see who you are. I have another meeting with one of our wolves in Washington, and then one with the Aspen Pack."

And with that, they were dismissed.

"The Aspen Pack?" Shane asked as they made their way back to the house. Only Shane lived there for now, but Bram had a feeling soon, all three would be staying there. That meant they would have to make it a home, not just a place to sleep.

Bram cleared his throat, focusing on Shane's question. "It's another Pack on this side of the country." He frowned as they walked inside the house, closing the door behind them. "I don't know much about them other than they're even more secretive than we are and kind of assholes."

Shane chuckled roughly. "I guess the same could be said about you guys from an outsider's perspective."

Bram tilted his head and growled. "Watch it, soldier. You're one of us now."

The puzzled look on Shane's face turned to a bright smile. "Yeah, I guess I am." The other man's eyes darkened, and he licked his lips. "And since we're alone..."

Bram barked out a laugh. "I'm thinking this new body of yours is showing you just how much stamina you have."

"My turn." That was all Shane said before the other man crushed his mouth to Bram's.

Bram growled low, biting and kissing, even as they both tore each other's clothes off. This would be no sweet and simple mating. This would be teeth and heat and claws. He wanted to hurt, wanted to feel the other man deep inside him even as he begged for release.

Shane looked down at his hands as he tore his mouth away, his eyes wide. "Fuck. They're claws."

It was just his fingertips, but that was enough to tell Bram that Shane needed to cool down a bit while he learned control. The fact that Shane had only shifted his fingertips and not anything else during the crazed passion told Bram that Shane's wolf was going to be as strong as hell.

Maybe Gideon and Kade were right, and there *were* stronger wolves now than there had been before because there was a reason for it.

"Breathe and picture yourself pulling your claws in. You can do this, Shane. You're in control."

Shane kept his gaze on Bram and focused. Soon, the claws were gone and in their place were two fists stiff with tension. Bram sighed and cupped the back of Shane's head, kissing him gently. Perhaps this wasn't the time for something rough.

Seeming to know where Bram's thoughts were going, Shane nipped at his lip. "Don't go soft on me." The other man cupped Bram, and a wicked gleam filled his eyes. "Okay, maybe you're not *too* soft, but don't be gentle. I'm learning. I've got this."

Bram inhaled deeply, letting the heady scent of Shane and his wolf wash over him. Bram could handle Shane, even if the other man lost control, and Shane was right—he needed to practice restraint.

And if both of them got off in the process, well, that was just fucking fantastic.

Bram went to his knees and licked his lips. "I'm going to make you come, but you can't let your claws come out. When you have more control, you can have them slide out during sex, but for now, you need to rein it in." They were already naked, and Shane's cock was hard, long, and thick. Bram stroked him once before licking the tip. "Can you do that?"

Shane slid his hand over Bram's head. "If you keep looking at me like that with my dick in your mouth, then, yeah, I'll be able to keep my claws in because I'm going to come in like two seconds."

Bram liked the sound of that and swallowed the man whole. He cupped Shane's balls, rolling them in his hand as he bobbed his head. And when the other man moaned, he used his free hand to reach around and rub Shane's prostate. There wasn't any lube around, so his saliva was going to have to do. But from the way Shane stiffened before coming down Bram's throat, it hadn't been an issue.

Bram's cock ached, and he needed to come, but he wasn't sure either of them was ready to go farther than they had just then. Shane was a little too close to his wolf, and they'd made love the night before. Though wolves could heal quickly, he didn't know how sore Shane was, and Bram wasn't sure Shane had the energy to fuck him like he needed him to.

The choice, however, was out of his hands when Shane slid to the floor, kissed Bram hard, and forced him to his back.

"I'll fuck you tonight," Shane said with a grin. "But for now, I need you in my mouth."

Bram groaned, sliding his hands through Bram's hair as Shane went down on him. The other man had a wicked tongue, and before he knew it, he was coming.

Sweaty and sated, the two of them ended up naked, wrapped around one another on the hardwood floor. They probably should have moved to a bed or even the couch, but Bram was too wrung out to care.

When a very sweet scent hit his nose, he smiled.

"I see you two have been busy," Charlotte said with a smile. "Can I join in?"

Bram looked over at Shane, who grinned. "I guess I'm not too tired, after all."

He knew that soon, their mating wouldn't only be about sex, and hell, it wasn't now. But their mating heat rode them hard, and he was so fucking happy to have the two of him in his arms, he could freely push thoughts of the uncertainty surrounding them out of his mind.

The real world would intrude soon enough, but for now, he could relax...for now, he could be Bram.

****

Shane stood with Charlotte near the Alpha's home, breathing in and out. She wanted him to learn how to bring his wolf close to the surface without shifting, *and* stay in control, and it wasn't easy. Bram was with the Redwoods, working his shift. They weren't sure how long he'd be an enforcer there, but he would still be doing his duty for as long as possible. Gideon was in and out of the house, working on a million things, but Charlotte had wanted the two of them close to the Alpha, just in case.

While she was Shane's mate, she wasn't his Packmate yet, and according to her, things could get tricky.

And he'd rather kill himself than hurt her because of his lack of control. Yet other than that one time with Bram and his claws, he was doing pretty well according to the others. He supposed he had to take that and run with it since he didn't quite feel like he was landing on his feet yet.

"You doing okay?" Charlotte asked. She slid her hand into his, and Shane smiled.

"Yeah, but with you so close and all bitable, I kind of want to forget the breathing I'm doing here and do some heavy breathing instead."

Charlotte winced. "That was...well, I don't know what that was, but that wasn't a line."

Shane wiped his mouth with his hand and tried to look chagrined. "Yeah, not one of my best."

"Just do better next time, and I'll give you a blowjob."

She said it so deadpan that it took a moment for the words to register. Shane threw his head back and laughed. He was falling for this woman, just as much as he was falling for Bram. It wasn't the bond that made him fall either. It was who they were, and how they fit with him. He'd known from the moment they'd walked into the infirmary room that they were different.

And now he knew why.

"What's so funny?" Gideon asked as he strolled toward them.

Shane was about to answer when he heard something. He wasn't sure what it was, but a sense of knowing slid over him. He jumped pulling both Charlotte and Gideon to the ground.

The explosion shocked the sky, the wards above them radiating a kaleidoscope of colors as they burned away the remnants of the bomb that had been thrown at them. But as Shane looked up, he knew that wouldn't be the end of it. Small cracks were forming in the wards. Not large enough to do anything at the moment, but those cracks would grow, and the wards would fall.

And then there would be nowhere safe for the wolves.

Gideon pushed him off, as did Charlotte, and the two of them stood. "You two okay?" Gideon growled.

"Yes," they both answered.

"Good. Now don't fucking risk your life for me again," Gideon growled.

"You're the Alpha," Shane growled right back. "If you die, our Pack might not make it. And *they* know that. I'm not going to let you die on my watch."

Something came and went in Gideon's eyes, and the other man nodded. Before he could say anything else, other wolves ran toward him—the Alpha's lieutenants. Each of them gave Shane a look he couldn't interpret, but he didn't think it was a bad thing, so he didn't respond other than to take Charlotte's hand in his.

"What happened?" Gideon asked. "And find our witches. See if they can help heal the cracks. Call the Redwoods and make sure they're okay."

Charlotte let out a little gasp. "I need to call my parents."

Gideon looked over at them. "Go, and report back to me."

Charlotte stiffened but didn't meet the Alpha's gaze. Gideon was full-on Alpha right now, but at the moment, he wasn't *her* Alpha. Shane wasn't sure exactly what that all meant, but he figured it had to be complicated.

"A helicopter flew over low and dropped a bomb on us," Kameron said as he stomped toward them. "They had to know they weren't going to take us out, but the point is, they *knew* where we were. And the fact that none of the guys in Washington warned us speaks volumes."

Gideon cursed.

"That means it was Montag," Shane added in, ignoring the way the others looked at him. He couldn't tell if they thought he was one of theirs or still the enemy, but he was past waiting on the sidelines. He would help any way he could. "If those wolves you have on the inside didn't now, then it wasn't a government operation. Montag is working outside the system, and he's fucking crazy. This is all him."

"Then it's retaliation." Gideon rubbed at his jaw and narrowed his eyes. "But it's not the end of it. This was just a test."

"So it seems." Kameron rolled his shoulders. "Ryder and Mitchell are out making sure everyone is okay, and Walker is ready to deal with any injuries. For now, it looks like it was just a loud explosion, but something else could be coming at any moment."

"Be on alert," Gideon ordered everyone within hearing distance. "This could be just the beginning."

But after four hours, they knew it had only been a test in a long game that no one wanted to play. Shane sank down in the tub fit for four and closed his eyes. His body hurt from shifting, nearly dying, and throwing his body around like he had. He was almost up to full strength, but he wasn't exactly there yet. Thank God he'd been in top shape before all of this had happened. If he hadn't been, he was sure he wouldn't be where he was now.

After they'd been on high alert for so long, Gideon had ordered Charlotte and Shane to rest. Bram was still with the Redwoods and would be for the night, leaving Shane and Charlotte by themselves. The Redwoods, thankfully, hadn't been attacked. Only the Talons. Only where Shane was now. That had to mean something, but Shane was too tired to think about it.

Of course, when Charlotte walked into the bathroom, naked, curvy, and fucking sexy as hell, Shane figured he wasn't too tired for everything.

Her hair covered her breasts, but her nipples peeked out from beneath the long waves. He loved her body, the way her hips flared out and her nipples went from a light brown to an even darker color when she was aroused. After he and Bram had sucked on them for hours, they turned even duskier.

Her breasts overfilled his hands, and he knew he'd never stop wanting to lick and bite every inch of her. He loved her ass, how it was firm but also round and perfect for his grip when he pounded into her.

He let out a groan, unable to hold it back and squeezed the base of his dick. "You're so fucking sexy, Charlotte."

She smiled at him then before cupping her breasts. "Oh, really?"

He licked his lips before slowly sliding his hand up and down his cock. He hadn't added any bubbles or shit to the water so she could see *exactly* what he was doing.

"Come closer but keep playing with your tits." She did as he ordered, and he lifted one hand out of the water. "Pinch your nipples. That's right. Do it hard and imagine it's me and Bram, taking turns, seeing who can make you come first."

"Goddess," she whispered. "You two are going to wear me out."

He slid his wet hand over her folds, pleased as fuck she was already damp for him. "We'll take care of you, Char. You know we will. Now spread your legs a bit so I can see your pretty pussy."

She spread for him.

Jesus, he was going to die a happy man. "I fucking love your cunt, baby. You're already wet for me and look how plump and swollen your folds are. Were you playing with yourself when you were out in the bedroom?" He brushed his knuckle along each side of her pussy before nudging it inside, just a tease.

Charlotte shook her head. "No. I wanted to come, but I'd rather have you do it for me."

He grinned then and used his thumb to gently scrape her clit. "That's my good girl. Come a little closer, baby. The tub is just the perfect height where if you put your leg on the edge, I can eat you out right here. You want that? You want my face between your legs and my mouth on your cunt? I love that sweet cream of yours on my tongue. You taste like ambrosia, and I have to lick every inch of you."

She moved her leg, and he shook his head. "I changed my mind. I don't want you to slip. Here, move to the edge of the tub, right on the rim. I want to fucking eat you up, baby. Can you let me do that?"

Charlotte let out a rough laugh. "I'm about to come from that dirty talk of yours alone, so yeah, I can do that. And Shane? I *really* want you to eat me out. So please, get to that."

Shane laughed. So this was what it was like to mate with a dominant female? He'd take it every fucking day if he could. She positioned herself at the edge of the tub and her feet dangled in the water. Shane went to his knees, not the most comfortable position in the tub, but he'd take it if he could taste her.

Charlotte spread her legs, putting her cunt on display, and Shane was actually glad he was on his knees. He could better pray to the moon goddess for this gift from here.

"Put your hands on the edge of the tub and keep yourself steady."

He didn't wait for her to respond; instead, he lowered his head and feasted. She *did* taste of ambrosia—sweet, delicate, and fucking *his*. He spread her with one hand and licked her from the bottom of her opening to her clit. With his other hand, he slid under her ass just a bit to play with her hole back there. Soon, he'd fill her ass with his cock, but for now, he'd make sure she could fit his fingers. Using her own juices, he massaged the area before sliding his finger into her hole.

She gasped and pressed her pussy closer to his face. He chuckled then, knowing the vibrations would go straight to her clit. Using his tongue and both hands, he fucked her pussy and her ass at the same time, and before long, she came hard, screaming his name.

Even as she was panting, her eyes glazed over in bliss, he stood up, gripped her hips, and flipped her over.

"Hold the edge of the tub." His voice was a low growl, and they were getting water everywhere. He knew it was probably fucking dangerous to fuck like this, but he needed to be in her.

Now.

She bent over, showing him that juicy ass and her very swollen pussy. He gripped the base of his cock and rammed into her in one stroke. They both froze, their breaths coming in pants.

"I think you just split me in half," Charlotte said with a laugh.

Shane immediately tried to pull out, but Charlotte gripped his wrist with one hand. "Did I hurt you? Fuck, baby. I'm sorry."

"Only the good kind of hurt. Now please, fuck me."

He snorted. "So nice of you to say please."

"Fine, if you're going to make fun of me..." She moved back along his cock before sliding off again. "I'll just fuck myself thank you very much."

Yep. Shane was a goner. There was no way he couldn't fall for the sexy woman, her humor, her strength...everything about her.

Shane gripped her hips, steadying her. "I'll take over, baby. Just stand there and enjoy."

She flipped him off, and he laughed. Soon, they were both moving, fucking each other and getting into the ideal rhythm. They were perfect for each other, not just in mating, but in the way they moved, the way they joked, and the way they thought about things.

He'd have been one lucky son of a bitch to find just her, and now he had her and Bram, too.

As he came, she clenched around him, coming, as well. She shook in his arms, and somehow, they both slid into the tub. He'd never been so grateful for the size of a bathtub in his life. He held her close, using his foot to turn on the faucet and add more hot water. He wanted to care for her, make sure she was okay and sated. From the look in her eyes, she was past sated and reveling in the same gluttony of pleasure he was.

Had he known he would find these two if he'd searched for them, he'd have done it in a heartbeat. As it was, he'd almost had to die, and had had to change his life, betray his people—and possibly his country—in order for it to happen.

And yet, looking back, he'd do it all again.

He'd die a thousand deaths if he could come back and have this woman in his arms. And soon, *soon*, he'd be strong enough to tell her that. But for now, he held his Charlotte close and focused on her.

The war would be there tomorrow, and Shane would be as ready as he could be for it.

Charlotte was here now, and though Shane hadn't been prepared for the intensity of what he felt for her, for Bram, he wouldn't wish it away.

He had his everything.

And now it was time to fight for it.

CHAPTER THIRTEEN

It almost felt weird being inside the Redwood wards after so much had happened at the Talons, but Charlotte knew she needed a while at home before she took the next step. She was mated, and while it was supposed to be a time for celebration, she knew they would have to wait to pop the champagne.

With the recent attack on the Talons, there hadn't been the opportunity to plan a true mating ceremony for them. And while they were bonded and technically blessed by both Alphas, they wouldn't have the ceremony to show off their new triad to the Packs until Charlotte and Bram were ready to become Talons.

The mating ceremony would have to wait, but for the first time, she was...happy.

She smiled more, she felt hot, sexy, and a little overly emotional at the thought that she finally had her best friend the way she should have all those months ago, and now they had this new man in their lives that completed their triad. Soon, they'd celebrate. But for now, in this time of war, they would train and protect their people. It was what her family had done during the Central war and now after the Unveiling, it was what they were forced to do, as well.

Charlotte put a hand over her stomach, worry racing through her. She hoped that one day her children would find mates and not have to deal with a war in their midst. Though she wasn't sure that would ever be an option. Not with how things were looking on either side of the line.

And that thought made her come up short. She needed to talk to one of the Healers about birth control. Now. She'd been an idiot in not using it before, but she hadn't had a reason to. First, they hadn't needed condoms when they'd been cementing the bonds as condoms wouldn't have prevented it in any case. Second, wolves didn't get sexually transmitted diseases so they were safe that way. However, in the following times, they could have gone to condoms, and she should have asked for the herbs the shifters used to prevent pregnancies.

But she hadn't been thinking.

But that would have to change now, as she didn't want to have a child yet. She wanted to learn who she was with Bram and Shane, as well as learn who they were with her. They had centuries to have children, and when they were ready, they would take that step. For now, she would take the herbs and hope they weren't too late. She wouldn't resent what had come from their mating—if anything had—but it wasn't exactly the best time for it.

"What are you worrying about over here?" Bram asked as he walked toward her.

She had been standing near her home, enjoying the breeze on her skin, but now, all she wanted to do was go inside and slam her best friend against the wall. She could blame it on the mating heat that always rode any mated pair—or triad—hard, but she had a feeling it had more to do with the man in front of her and not any magical connection.

The bond between them pulsed.

Okay, perhaps *some* of it was their magical connection.

She reached out to dance her fingers along his jaw. He raised a brow, standing still for her so she could play. She loved that he did that and so much more. He reminded her of a jungle cat sometimes, all sleek and powerful. Yes, he was a wolf, and comparing him to a cat would get her in trouble, but she didn't care. He stood still for her to touch his face, his shoulders, his chest. He always made sure she, and now Shane, were taken care of before he did anything for himself.

That's why she was glad she and Shane were on the same page when it came to taking care of Bram, rather than the other way around.

Someone needed to care for him and make sure his needs were met.

He might be dominant in bed and in life, but when it came to those he cared about, he wasn't forceful. He was the quiet dominant wolf, and those were the ones you usually had to watch out for.

And now he was hers.

"Are you going to tell me what you're thinking about? Or should I guess?"

She traced her fingertips along his lips after he'd spoken and shook her head. "I'm only thinking about you. Come to bed with me." It was a whisper. A need laid bare before the man she loved. One of the men she loved.

How had she gotten here? How had this become her life?

Warmth filled her, and she smiled.

She was...happy.

For the first time since she'd seen Ellie and Maddox in that basement and they'd saved her life, she was past content and into pure joy. Was this what it felt like to be mates? Was this what it meant to have a future not wrapped up in darkness?

And maybe, just maybe, she deserved this.

Bram lowered his head and brushed his lips along hers. "I think that sounds like a perfect plan." He kissed her fully then, his tongue sliding along hers. She moaned into him and wrapped her arms around his neck.

This man. This was what she needed.

Him and Shane.

Forever.

He gripped her butt and lifted her off her feet. She chuckled and held on tightly, wrapping her legs around his waist. The position left the long line of his cock pressed firmly against her heat, and she sighed happily.

"Let's get inside before your whole family finds us naked and sweaty in the middle of the forest."

Once again, she traced his jaw with her finger a few times, even as he carried her into her house. "Well, I'd like to get naked and sweaty with you outside once, but yeah, in front of my family, not so much."

He grinned, and she fell in love with him all over again. Goddess, he had the most beautiful smile, and she prayed one day he would use it more often. He closed the door behind her and pushed her back against the wall.

With her body pinned and her legs wrapped around his waist to steady her, he pulled her arms up over her head so she was completely at his mercy.

And goddess, how she loved it.

If any other man or woman tried to pin her down, she'd fight, but Bram and Shane? It just made her want to wrap around them tightly and take all that they could give her.

"I'm going to fuck you against your door. What do you think about that?"

Charlotte smiled and arched her back, pressing her hips closer to his. "I think we're wearing too many clothes."

Bram raised a brow, and before she could ask him what he was going to do next, he was using his claws to rip her clothes from her body.

She moaned, in awe of how careful he was, even as he handled her roughly at the same time. His claws grazed her skin, but it was in a sensual move, not a violent one. And when she was naked, still against the door and panting, he held her with one arm and somehow slid out of his clothes, as well.

Now they were both naked, ready, and willing.

It was about time.

She closed her eyes as he slid his lips over her skin, his mouth working her shoulders, her breasts, her neck. She couldn't help but remember the last time they'd been alone like this. She'd been so happy, so...in love with the man in her arms, and too afraid to do anything about it once the worst happened. She'd wanted him to move on to find his own fate, and had hurt them both in the process.

She'd been wrong before, and she was damned if she'd do it again.

"Ouch!" she called out and opened her eyes. Bram glared at her, and she rubbed her nipple where he'd bitten down none too gently. "What was that for?"

"I'm doing some of my best work here, and you're frowning. What's going on in that head of yours?"

She shook her head. "I was just thinking about how we almost lost this." She cupped his face. "I'm not going to lose you again."

He turned his head to kiss her palm. "Damn straight." And when he kissed her, she lost all thoughts of what they'd been through before and only focused on what they had right then. He worked her until she was right at the edge and then slid into her. They panted as one, their bodies moving in unison as they made love. It was hard and yet soft at the same time, fast, and yet never-ending.

And when they came, they threw their heads back and howled, their mating bond once again flaring, cementing them as part of their third. Deep along the bond, she felt Shane's adoration of Bram and Charlotte together, and she couldn't wait to see him again. She'd only known him a short while, but somehow, he'd become a deeper part of her life, an integral one she knew she couldn't live without.

She had two mates, two paths wrapped into one, and a future she could taste on her tongue. Perhaps fate hadn't betrayed her when she'd been a child and then again when she'd been wrong about Bram. And now that she thought she could live with that, she could breathe again.

She had her best friend, her lover, her mate in her arms—along with Shane waiting close by—and for now, and perhaps for eternity, that would be enough.

"Do you see that?" Charlotte asked Chloe as they patrolled the Redwood and Talon border. There was a clearing of neutral ground that each Pack guarded as one. It had once been part of the Central Pack territory, she knew, and she tried not to think too hard about that.

Chloe, a Talon member who was right out of juvenile status, frowned. "It looks like a fallen log, but not really."

On alert, Charlotte texted the coordinates to the Redwood Enforcer as Chloe did the same to the Talon's.

"Something is off about this," she whispered. "I'd wait to see what it is, but it's near the human path that hikers take daily now. If they get too close, and it's not just a log..."

"Let's check it out," Chloe put in when Charlotte trailed off. "We can't just leave it there."

Charlotte nodded and moved forward. She took four steps and her wolf howled, warning her of what was to come.

The log that wasn't a log exploded, sending thousands of pieces of shrapnel toward them. She held back a scream as wood and metal pierced her body, cutting her deeply in places. She reached out for Chloe, but knew it was too late. The other woman turned as she fell to the ground, her eyes wide, her neck cut from side to side from a large piece of metal.

Charlotte hit the ground moments after the fallen woman, trying to get her bearings. She growled, her wolf ready to fight, but something smashed her on the back of the head. She only had a moment to wonder what it was, what had come from the wrong direction to hit her, before everything went black.

And she was gone.

****

Bram almost fell to his knees as the shock rocked along the bond. Bile filled his throat, and a metallic taste coated his tongue. His ears rang, and his wolf howled, scraping along his skin, begging to be let out. The wolf needed blood, needed flesh beneath its claws.

It needed revenge for whatever the hell had made the bond twist and bend the way it had just then. It hadn't broken, no, but it had been damn close to doing so.

Shane, not yet at full strength, sagged against him. He lifted his mate up slightly, and the other man shook him off, standing straight once again.

"What the hell was that?" Shane asked, his eyes wide.

"Charlotte," Bram bit out, his breath ragged. "Something happened to Charlotte."

His phone buzzed then, and he pulled it out, his hands shaking like crazy. He usually had way more control than this, but he could barely breathe when it came to Charlotte.

He read the screen and cursed. "It's Kade. I need to go to the neutral territory. Apparently, Charlotte sent out coordinates of something suspicious right before we felt that pain along the bond."

"I'm going with you." Shane was almost fully healed from the shift, but he didn't have a lot of training at being wolf.

It didn't matter, though. Not when their mate was in danger.

"Let's go."

In the end, it took longer than merely running at full speed toward the coordinates Charlotte had left. Gideon and the others had stopped them on their way out, alerted that their wolf, Chloe, was out of contact, as well.

Fear edged along Bram's spine, and he did his best to ignore it. He couldn't function if he were lead by fear alone. Anger and determination he could work with, but not mind-numbing fear. Shane hadn't said another word after they'd told the Talon Alpha what they knew. Instead, the other man shifted from foot to foot while they waited, and then, in the car ride over, had fisted his hands on his tense thighs, his gaze focused as he went through whatever he needed to in his head.

Bram had seen the man work before, but this was a new kind of intensity. Shane was a soldier, through and through, and now he was wolf besides. Meaning everything he did from now on would have a new power behind it.

They would need that, Bram feared. That and so much more in the time to come.

As soon as they reached the neutral territory, Bram and Shane hopped out of the vehicle. Kameron and Brandon had been in the front of the SUV and were right by their sides.

Another SUV pulled up almost at the same time, and Maddox, Ellie, and a couple of Redwood enforcers, including Quinn, hopped out.

"Where is she?" Maddox asked, his voice low. He was looking right at Bram. "Use the bond if you have to, but find my baby girl."

"Maddox," Ellie admonished. "Let's get to the site before you growl and go crazy."

Maddox's nostrils flared, but he nodded once at Bram, then Shane, before turning and following his mate.

Shane met Bram's eyes, his brows raised. "I guess those are her parents?" Though Charlotte had told Shane of her childhood and mentioned Maddox and

Ellie, Shane hadn't left the Talon den before this to actually meet the Redwoods.

Bram nodded. "Let's find our girl."

They ran to the place where Charlotte had last been, and he almost tripped when he saw the body lying in the rubble.

She was the wrong shape, her hair the wrong color, but he'd had a moment when he'd thought it was Charlotte.

Brandon let out a curse and fell to his knees beside the fallen wolf. Chloe. "Damn it. Damn it. Damn it."

Kameron bent down, as well, his jaw tense. He helped Brandon turn the woman over, and Bram sent a prayer to the goddess for her soul.

"Walker is on his way, got waylaid by a sick pup, but he'd have been too late," the Talon Enforcer growled. "Damn it. He'd have been too late." The other man closed his eyes and put his hand on Chloe's cheek. "Too damn young."

"What did this?" Brandon bit out.

"Someone left a bomb that wasn't too cleverly concealed over here. The center of the impact is here, and whoever made it shoved it full of a fuckton of shrapnel. Anyone too close didn't have a chance."

Bram looked over at Shane as the other man spoke. "She's still alive, Shane. We can feel her. But where is she? She wouldn't just leave Chloe right here out in the open if she could help it."

"We can feel her too, along the Pack bonds," Maddox put in. "But where is she? I'm not the Omega anymore. I can't find her like I used to." He turned to Bram then. "Find her. Use the bond and find her."

Bram ran a hand over his face. "You think I don't want that? I don't know *how*. Not all bonds work the same."

Shane stalked toward them, his hands shaking by his side. "I don't know what I'm doing, but I'm going to find your daughter."

Ellie raised her chin, her wolf in her eyes. "I know you will. We all will." She reached out and cupped Shane's face, surprising the other man from the way his eyes widened. "The bond is always different, but try at least. Close your eyes and picture the bond. Then travel along that thread, follow each path it takes, and try to sense her. You're not going to get a perfect picture, but maybe you'll get a feeling. Your bond is still so new, it's finding its place amid the bonds of the Pack. It can do extraordinary things right now, and perhaps even more later. Just try, Shane. Find my baby."

Bram let out a breath, and something caught his eye. Blood stained a large rock that didn't look like it had come from the bomb itself. In fact, it looked like it had fallen *over* pieces of the bomb material.

He frowned, kneeling near it. Charlotte's scent hit him full force, and his wolf came to the surface. A growl ripped from his throat, and his claws tore through his fingertips.

"Someone hit her over the head it seems with this rock," he bit out. The words were hard to form, and he knew he was far too close to shifting for comfort. He took deep breaths and reined in his wolf. Brandon put his hand on Bram's shoulder, and though the other man wasn't *his* Omega, he was his mate's, and somehow, the other man helped him. He wasn't sure if it was some trick of the bonds or the fact that Brandon just had a steadying presence. Either way, he was grateful. "Thanks."

"No problem," Brandon said softly. "It's what I do."

Bram looked over his shoulder at Shane, who still had his eyes closed, his features focused.

"Someone took Charlotte," Bram said after a moment. "That's the only answer. I don't know who, and I don't know why, but we're going to find her."

Kameron rubbed his chin. "It all smells like a trap to me."

"Then we'll get trapped," Bram said simply. "But I'm not going to let them have her because we're too scared to do anything about it."

Kameron's eyes rose, and the bastard smiled. "I'm going to like having you as a Talon, I think. And yeah, we're going to find her. Montag isn't going to win. Ever."

"You think it's Montag?" Bram asked.

"It's his calling card," Shane answered instead. "And I'm pretty sure Kameron here has been studying Montag's moves for a while now."

"Better to know your enemy than be surprised by it," the Talon Enforcer answered.

"I think I can find her," Shane put in at that moment.

Bram turned quickly to face his mate. "You can?"

Shane nodded, his eyes cloudy. "I think you can, too. Just do what Ellie said and *try*. We'll find her, damn it. There isn't another option."

Bram leaned forward and kissed the other man hard on the lips. "No, there isn't. We're going to find her. I know it."

Because if they didn't, he'd lose everything all over again. And he wasn't sure he and Shane would survive without her.

CHAPTER FOURTEEN

Charlotte needed to wake up. Pain radiated through her skull, knocking around so it felt like someone had bashed her head in. And if she thought about it that might be the case, but she honestly didn't know anymore. Her eyes were too heavy, and while the rest of her body hurt even more than her skull, she knew she couldn't do anything about it until she *woke up.*

Wake up, Charlotte. Wake up.

No amount of chanting would work, though. And her wolf was *too* quiet.

Fear began to crawl icily through her body, and she did her best to ignore it. Fear wouldn't get her out of this situation—a situation she didn't even know the root of as of yet.

So yes, she needed to wake up.

Muffled voices surrounded her, and she stiffened, her mind slowly working its way to being fully conscious. She tried to open her eyes, but again, they were too heavy, but she was getting closer and closer to being able to see what was going on.

She couldn't sense her Pack or any other wolves around her, and that was what brought on the fear. Those voices she heard weren't Pack. They had to belong to whoever had knocked her over the head and most likely taken her away from where the bomb had thrown her down—where Chloe had lost her life.

At that thought, her wolf whimpered a bit, as if waking up from a dazed coma herself. A sense of relief poured through Charlotte for only a moment before she tamped it down. She could feel that when she was home in her mates' arms, and when those who *dared* to harm her and take Chloe's life were punished.

Preferably with their throats slit just like the young wolf's, who had died before Charlotte's eyes.

Finally, she cracked open her lids and winced at the harsh lighting. She tried to lick her dry and chapped lips but froze when she realized that there were dark shadows blocking some of the lights above her.

They were watching.

"Good," a deep voice, a *familiar* voice, exclaimed. "You're awake. I was afraid the men had hit you too hard, and we'd lost you before we had a chance to use you."

Montag.

This was General Montag. Though, was he still a General if he'd gone rogue? The military *had* to know one of their own had gone off his rocker by now, but she wasn't sure what anyone was going to do about it right then. The "shifter problem" was on everyone's minds, and apparently, no one could work fast enough to take care of one of their own, a demented man with too much power.

Charlotte held back the rush of breath she wanted to exhale as she brought her thoughts back into focus. She needed to worry about the problem at hand and not everything else going on, but her head hurt too much for her to think clearly yet.

Hopefully, she'd heal enough to figure it out soon, or it might be too late.

Her eyes finally opened fully, and she held her breath. Four men and one woman stood around her, all dressed in dark military outfits that bore no insignia. They were truly off the grid it seemed, and that didn't bode well for her at all.

The room had been painted the normal eggshell white of most hospital or clinic rooms with metal cabinets and countertops glistening under the harsh lights. Someone had strapped her down with thick rubber and metal bands to a long medical table so she couldn't move. Whoever had designed the straps knew how to keep shifters contained, and that scared her but didn't surprise her. After all, she'd known Montag had tortured and studied other wolves at his previous lab before Shane and the rest of them had blown it up.

Charlotte figured she was now in their new headquarters and lab.

Fear once again tried to crawl up her spine, but she ignored it. Montag and his goons surrounding her needed her full attention, and her worries had no place here.

Montag reached out and gripped her face in his hand, pinching her cheeks and chin. If she hadn't already been dazed, strapped down to a metal table, and bleeding from the bomb that had sent shrapnel into her skin, she could have fought him off.

But because she wasn't at her full strength, he could try to intimidate her and do whatever he wanted.

She'd be damned if she let him for long, though.

"I know exactly who you are, Charlotte Jamenson. But you used to be Charlotte Reyes, isn't that right?

The daughter of the former Central Pack Alpha. He kept you chained in his basement, didn't he? Or was that your brother, the man who took over after your father met with an...unfortunate accident."

He nodded over her head at another person, who came into view. The man in black held out a metal cuff too large for a wrist or ankle.

She knew *exactly* what that was for.

They were going to make her relive what she'd endured as a child, and perhaps even more. Charlotte stiffened, then cursed herself for letting this man see anything about what she was feeling. She'd *known* some of the government knew about each of the Packs and had kept it secret. But she hadn't really thought this one man would know so much about her past.

And if he knew about her past, then he knew her weaknesses.

And for a man who had her in his clutches, that would be exactly what he needed to break her.

I won't break.

I am strong. I am Charlotte Jamenson. I am mated to Bram and Shane. I am Pack. I am loved. I am me.

I will not break.

"You're also the daughter of Maddox Jamenson, isn't that right?" Montag slid his finger down her cheek, and bile rose in her throat.

"Fuck you," she spat.

His grip tightened. "That's not the kind of experiments we do here. Fortunately for you. And I think you would do well to remember who came before you. Isn't that right? Maddox has a scar right on his cheek, one that never healed because of some magic or whatever you wolves call it. Well, we don't have magic, but I have something special that will make sure you never heal." He studied her face, his own impassive. "That is, if you live long enough for it to scar."

She wouldn't let them kill her, wouldn't let them take everything she had.

Shane and Bram would come for her.

Her family would come for her.

And damn it, she would save herself, as well.

She thrashed under the straps, putting all her weight and strength into the struggle, trying to break free. The others in the room might have weapons, but she *was* a weapon. Even weak, if she were fast enough—and damn it, she was *always* fast—she'd be able to take them out even if they hurt her in the process.

She just needed to get out of the prison they held her in.

"Why are you doing this?" she asked, her wolf in her voice. "Do you get off on cutting up women who can't fight back?"

Montag looked like he wanted to hit her but held himself back. Instead, he released her and wiped his hand over her clothes as if he couldn't stand the scent of her on his skin. Good, because she wanted nothing to do with him.

"I want the man you call your mate."

His gaze locked with hers when her eyes widened. "Yes, I know much more than you think. I saw the way you leaned into him and that other man on the feed when you blew up my compound. You think I'd have left it without someone watching it beyond those guards you took out? You aren't as smart as you think you are. I want Shane back, and now that I have you, he'll come right to me. I would have preferred not to have to bother with you, but the man refused to leave the den. He didn't even budge when we tested the wards."

He had to be talking about the bomb they'd dropped right on top of the den that the wards had barely been able to hold back. But even as her mind worked through that, she could only think of one thing.

Shane.

Montag wanted Shane.

Of course, the man wanted Shane. Her mate was the only thing left of Montag's experiments. At least, that was what they had thought before, and from the manic way the former General was acting now, she had a feeling the Packs had been right. Montag needed Shane's blood to continue his experiments.

Only the other man didn't know the serum hadn't worked. It had only brought Shane closer to what he could have been if he'd been bitten. The whole process had almost killed him multiple times, and the ramifications of a man-made serum being introduced into the Pack bonds weren't even known yet. This human, this Montag, had forever changed the Packs, yet he didn't even know it.

She wouldn't be telling him, though. Giving him that much information would be deadly.

And if they didn't take care of him and make a stand, she knew her people would never have a fighting chance. They would forever be throwing new ways to torture at them and take them out in any way they could.

"While we wait for Shane to show up so I can get what I need from his blood, we might as well begin."

He tilted his head, studying her, and she wanted to punch him in his too smug face. "This should be interesting." But he didn't stay to see what would become of her. Instead, he left, taking one of his men with him.

Maddox and Ellie had been through something like this before when they'd first been mated, and their captivity was how they'd found Charlotte and saved her life. When the human male put the collar around her neck, chaining her to the wall behind her but still keeping her on the table, she knew she'd come full circle.

But she wouldn't let the others save her this time. Instead, she would save herself.

It was the only way to make sure Montag never got his hands on Shane.

The woman who had been standing at the edge of the table came forward then, her hand outstretched, and Charlotte held back a growl. The knife in her hand was coated with something, and she couldn't sense what it was, but it couldn't be good.

She let out a low breath, relaxing her body as much as she could. It would take almost every ounce of her strength to do what she needed to do next.

The woman passively placed the knife on Charlotte's temple, and that's when Charlotte *moved*. The blade dug in, and excruciating pain slammed into her. But instead of weakening her, she pushed through the pain, letting it help her. With all of her strength, she pushed up with all four limbs at the same time, using her claws to cut through what she could.

Once she got through the rubber that had been touching her skin, she screamed. They had coated the chains with the same substance they had the knife, but she pushed through it and got her arm out of the strap.

She was one of the fastest wolves out there, and right then, she knew she was faster than she'd ever been before.

Her hand shot out and took the knife from the other woman. Before the soldier could gasp, Charlotte had stabbed the other woman through the neck with the blade and rolled off the table. Her body was bloody, cut up, and she wasn't healing yet thanks to the multiple shrapnel wounds and whatever had been on those chains.

She *knew* she'd bear these marks forever, as well as the one on her temple from where the knife had dug in, but it didn't matter.

Charlotte would not be bound.

She would not be caged.

She would fight. And she would be free.

And she would kill anyone in her way.

****

Shane's blood boiled, but he didn't growl, didn't scream, didn't say a word. Instead, he focused deep inside on that tiny thread that connected him to the two people who had become the most important things in his world.

"Turn left here," Bram growled out. "We're getting closer."

Kameron turned and let out a breath. "I wish I had the ability to use a GPS tracker like the two of you seem to have right now."

Shane let out a breath. "I hope you mean in general, because I wouldn't wish this feeling of being so out of your depths you can't breathe on anyone if they're trying to find their mate."

Kameron met Shane's eyes, a newfound respect shining in them. "Truer words..." the other man whispered. "We're going to find your mate, damn it. We're not going to let Charlotte be hurt."

Bram, who was in the front seat, kept silent at the exchange as Walker shifted slightly next to Shane in the back seat.

"I still can't believe you got Maddox and Ellie to stay behind and go back to their den," the Healer said.

Shane focused on the frail bond again as Bram spoke. "We all know this is a trap of some kind. Everyone was needed back at their dens since we don't know which one they could attack. And they trusted us to find their daughter and bring her home."

He couldn't formulate words as to how much that trust meant to him. They'd all agreed that it would be too much to have her parents *and* her mates there just in case emotions got the best of them and it hurt their escape plan or distracted their fighting. As the three of them were so newly mated, it made sense for Bram and Shane to go and her parents to stay behind. But if they didn't find her within a certain time limit, Maddox and Ellie would be leading the charge to find their daughter.

"She's close," Bram breathed. "We should stop here and go the rest of the way on foot just in case."

Kameron stopped the car and tilted his head. "There are humans around." His voice was a low growl. "And since there isn't a town on the map, I have a feeling we're going to need to fight our way in."

Shane cracked his knuckles. "Good."

They formulated a plan and got out of the SUV quietly. Though he wasn't as trained as the others when it came to using all of his new senses, he was still a former elite soldier and could carry his weight.

They crept through the forest, and he ignored the sound of the wind in the trees and the animals going deathly quiet around four large predators within their midst. It was only a two-minute hike. But with each step closer to Charlotte, Shane felt as if it took far longer.

When they got to the edge of a clearing, the four stopped and crouched down behind a large row of bushes to look at the structure up ahead.

She was in there. He could feel it.

He looked over to mouth something to the others, then shot his attention back to the doorway of the large grey building in front of them.

"Holy hell," Kameron whispered. "Your mate is one fucking tough wolf."

Shane let out a growl, and the four of them moved as one to make sure Charlotte would be able to make it out completely. Blood covered her from head to toe, and she gripped a crimson tipped knife in her hand. She was about a quarter of a mile away, but he could see her clearly.

He couldn't tell exactly where she was hurt, but his wolf howled to get closer.

"Get the guards on the side that are coming for her, Shane," Bram ordered. "I'll get the ones on the other side if Kameron can get the ones in the middle. Walker? Get Charlotte out of here." Bram paused. "No survivors. Not this time. We can't."

It echoed Gideon's and Kade's earlier assessment, and Shane knew things were changed once again.

Though Shane didn't want anyone else to take Charlotte, he knew Walker would be the best bet as it looked as if she desperately needed a Healer. As soon as the final words had left Bram's mouth, the three of them were off, taking care of what they needed to.

The three men on the side of the building Shane ran to were familiar.

Too familiar.

He'd fought alongside these men, battled insurgents by their side when they'd been in war. He'd saved their lives, and he knew they had done the same for him. They had been his brothers in arms, and he'd thought brothers of his soul.

He had been wrong.

Oh so fucking wrong.

When he came into their line of sight, they looked shocked for a moment then raised their guns to shoot.

The betrayal of that action slapped at Shane, but he ignored it. They had betrayed their country, betrayed Shane, and betrayed their own sense of honor.

He was a wolf now, and had a new set of priorities that should have aligned with those in front of him, but not any longer. These men had signed their death warrants, and Shane would do what he had to in order to protect his people.

Before the soldiers could get off the first round, he had one guy down, his neck snapped. Shane's wolf was at the surface, guiding him as he learned to blend his old knowledge with his newly developed skills.

He took down the other two easily enough, though one bullet did graze him. It burned like hell, but he ignored it. After taking a look around and deciding that was the last of them for now, he went back to the front of the building to see if he could help.

The others had been busy, their wolves in their eyes as he made their way to them. Walker was on the ground, Charlotte in his arms as he worked on Healing some of her wounds.

Shane went to his knees at Walker's side. "Char," he bit out.

She smiled painfully at him. "I got out myself." She words were hoarse, and he couldn't help the pride that flowed through him.

"Hell yeah, you did."

"We need to get out of here," Kameron growled as Bram hurried toward them. Relief covered Shane's mate's face for a moment before he was all wolf once again. "I don't know how many others are in the building or who could be coming. We don't have any time."

Walker picked up Charlotte and held her close. "I'm not her Healer, and my magic shouldn't be working at all, but it is enough that she should be good until we get her to the Redwood Healer or until Gideon brings her into the Talons. The mating bond with you is making things a little funky, but I've stopped most of the bleeding."

Charlotte sighed and reached out for Shane. "Get me to the Talon den and I'll let Gideon finish it. We have to go."

Shane's wolf howled with purpose, and he kissed Charlotte's bloodstained hand before squeezing it. "Let's get you home."

They were sitting ducks where they stood, but Charlotte was safe for now. She'd somehow saved herself, and for that, he knew she would always have a renewed sense of worth within herself she might have doubted before.

But things weren't over. Montag had to be creeping around, perhaps even watching them now, and that meant they needed to *move*. Shane wouldn't feel safe until they were within their den wards, surrounded by his Pack and those he trusted.

As they ran back to the SUV in order to head to the Talons, he let those words filter through his brain. So much had changed since he'd first learned of the shifters, and yet, he knew this was how it was always supposed to be.

Before he had been a soldier because that had been the only thing he imagined he could be. He'd formed connections to others, but never as strong as they could have been. Now he was a wolf, mated to a man and a woman he knew he loved, though he had yet to say the words. And he was on the run from a man he had thought he respected enough to die for in the heat of battle because things were never as he thought they were.

His world had shifted, and yet he knew he could live with the outcome.

He just prayed that he would live long enough in the end to make sure the others knew it had been worth it to become wolf the way he had.

The war was here, and they were on the front lines.

And no matter what, Shane would do *anything* to protect his Pack and those he loved.

Anything.

ELEVENTH HOUR

"It's not over," Montag spat. "It can't be over." He looked into his tablet at the man on the screen and cursed.

McMaster shrugged and looked as if he hadn't a care in the world, as if their plan with the shifters hadn't just failed spectacularly. They were on a secure channel that they had both assured themselves was unhackable, so they were able to speak freely.

Of course, McMaster never spoke too freely. He always spoke in half-truths, and it pissed off Montag to no end. The other man was too polished, too squeaky-clean for the cameras he loved so much.

Montag hated working with him, but he was desperate. The female wolf shouldn't have been able to get out as she had, and because of his fucking weak crew, he'd lost his final asset.

"You tried, and you failed." McMaster waved his hand. "You're done for, Montag. You're on your own here."

"You fucking bastard."

McMaster raised a pristine brow he probably had waxed weekly. "Watch your words."

Montag slammed his fists onto his desk. "You made promises, McMaster. You're going to help me finish what we started."

"It's over," McMaster said cooly. "You're on your own." He cut off the feed, and Montag threw his tablet against the wall.

He needed McMaster to help with his part of the deal, or Montag would have to take things to the next level.

He wasn't sure the world was ready for that.

But if he had to, he'd watch the world burn before he let it go into the hands of the mongrels who called themselves part human.

He'd do what he must.

He'd make the final strike.

And when the wolves went to their knees in surrender...he'd kill them.

All of them.

No mercy. No weakness. No more wolves.

Not even the one he thought he could make.

Not even Shane.

CHAPTER FIFTEEN

The car ride was excruciating, but Bram could do nothing but sit in the front seat and look back at his mates. Walker worked to Heal Charlotte as much as he could without technically being bonded to her as Healer to Packmember. Bram cursed himself for not having the Redwood Healer with them, but they hadn't had the time to grab Mark and bring him along.

As it was, Walker was doing as much as he could, and as *soon* as they saw Gideon, they would become Talons. They'd waited for things to settle long enough. Bram's only family was Shane and Charlotte so while he would miss what he had before, he knew his future was with the Talons. And even though Charlotte had been holding off because of the family that had taken her in, even she had said it was time.

Soon, they would be Talons, and Charlotte would be able to be fully Healed from her ordeal.

And, hopefully, they would have enough time to do all of that before the shit hit the fan and Montag found them.

Charlotte let out a hiss, and Shane hovered over her since she was in his lap. Her feet were over Walker as the Healer did his best to do what he could. Bram hated being so far away from her, and because he couldn't think of anything else to bring her closer, he said the only thing he could.

"I love you, Charlotte. I'm so fucking proud of you. I love you so fucking much. You too, Shane. I'm sorry I didn't say it before. I love you both. Thought you ought to know since I almost waited too long as it was."

The noise in the SUV dropped at his words, and Shane barked out a confused laugh. "Well, this seems as good a time as any to say I love you both. I was going to wait until we weren't covered in blood and bruises but that doesn't seem to be often."

Both Walker and Kameron snorted, but Bram only had eyes for Charlotte.

Tears slid down her cheeks, but she gave him a watery smile. "I love you both, you know. You should have figured that out already." She inhaled. And now that we've embarrassed our poor Healer and Enforcer, let's talk about all of that later. Okay?"

"I kind of like how she said our," Kameron said with a grin. The man didn't grin often, so Bram was surprised to see it. "The Pack is going to love having you. I'd feel bad that the Redwoods are going to lose you, but they took our sister since she mated Finn, and they took Quinn, too, so I'm kind of over it."

Bram opened his mouth to say something, but the SUV braked quickly, and he braced himself. "What?" He turned in his seat and cursed.

They were right outside the Talon den, and the wards were holding, but...

It seemed Montag had worked fast.

Too fast.

And they weren't alone.

Montag had brought a fucking *tank* to a battle with wolves. He must have had everything locked up and ready to go the moment he needed to attack the Talon den. And while the wolves could hide behind the wards, Bram knew they wouldn't. Not with the barrier as weak as it was. With the humans knowing that shifters existed, the magic that helped feed the wards was slowly fading away.

And because Gideon knew this, many of the Talon's strongest were already outside the wards, ready to fight those who had come to take over their Pack.

"We need to help them," Charlotte pleaded, breaking the silence.

"Absolutely not," Bram growled. "You were just fucking *tortured*. You need to get behind the wards and stay safe."

"Fuck you, Bram. If you think I can do that, then you don't know me at all."

Had it only been a few moments ago that they'd declared their love for each other? This was what happened when three dominant wolves mated.

"Well, I don't think we're going to have a lot of time to make a different decision," Shane put in, his attention on what was going on outside the vehicle. The SUV was hidden behind a group of trees, but Bram knew they couldn't hide forever. "Montag's people are moving forward."

"We need to move," Kameron ordered. "Walker, get ahold of the Redwoods just in case the others haven't been able to. Charlotte, you stay beside Shane the entire time. Got me? You're both not up to a hundred percent, but you're better together. Bram? You're with me. Let's go."

Thankful the other man had a plan, but still slightly bristling at the orders, Bram hopped out of the SUV behind the others. Before they could head off in their respective directions, however, Bram tugged Shane to him, kissing him full on the mouth.

"I love you, do you understand that? You don't get to die on me tonight, not when I just found you." He kissed Shane again, aware the others were staring him. Yes, Bram didn't speak often, but when he did, it *mattered*.

He turned and pulled Charlotte gently to his chest, kissing her softly. When he pulled back, his wolf was close to the surface, ready for what was next. "Protect him. Protect yourself. Believe in who you are. You are one of the *best* wolves I know, and I know you can do anything. But don't fucking die on me. I love you, Charlotte." He kissed her again before watching his two mates leave to their positions along with Walker while he let his wolf come even closer to the surface.

"Let's do this," Kameron growled.

"Till the end," Bram agreed.

The explosion rang in his ears, and Bram growled. As soon as he and Kameron had gotten to Gideon's side, the Alpha let his wolf into his eyes and slashed his palm. Bram did the same to his and slammed his hand to Gideon's.

His Pack bond to the Redwood severed; the feeling of being sucked into a vacuum forcing him almost to his knees before the mating bond wrapped around him, anchoring him until the Talon Pack bond slammed into place, bringing him into the fold. This new Pack was rougher than his old one, it tasted different, smelled of other scents he didn't understand, but he didn't care.

He'd learn this new bond and this new Pack later.

For now, he would fight alongside them, bleed with them, show them that he was now theirs. And because he was a Talon, Walker would be able to Heal him fully if needed, and the Alpha and others would have Bram's immense strength during the battle.

"Thank fuck," Gideon growled. "I already brought Charlotte in. Now, let's do this. Brie is behind the wards because she's pregnant, but you know damn well she'd be fighting next to Charlotte if she could."

"Understood." And he did, though he honestly wanted everyone safe and wrapped in cotton wool at the moment.

"What are they saying? Why are they here?" Kameron asked.

Gideon growled under his breath. "They showed up here right before you did. They must have had the fucking *tank* concealed and on a truck of some kind. They haven't said anything, but I guess actions speak louder than words."

"We're fighting," Bram said. It wasn't a question, but Gideon answered anyway.

"We're fighting."

Again, the explosion rang out in his ears, but it wasn't from the new bond. Montag attacked first, his people coming at them with guns and knives. The wolves were faster, but only just.

Because this wasn't the full force of the government and only Montag's people, there weren't as many humans as there could have been. But there were still twice as many as there were wolves on the field. The Redwoods were on the way, but they might not get there in time.

Bullets sprayed past Bram's head as he fought two soldiers, hand-to-hand. Gideon fought at his side, the Alpha a force to be reckoned it. Bram rolled to the ground as a brown-haired man slammed into his side. He kicked at the other man, and Gideon pulled on Bram's shoulder, helping him to his feet.

Bram growled, his claws out. He fought next to his Alpha, battling not only for his life but also for his people, his Pack. No matter how many people they fought, more kept coming. Bram honestly started to worry they might never find an ending to this.

Beside them, Brandon fell to the ground. A bullet had hit the Omega's side. Gideon growled even louder, and Bram did the only thing he could do: he protected his Alpha.

He wasn't an enforcer anymore, but he would damn well act like a lieutenant and keep his new Alpha alive.

Parker, who had been at the Talons to speak to Gideon, went to Brandon's side, helping the other man up. Brandon yelled at him, and Bram couldn't tell what it was about. The other wolves shouted at one another, Parker trying to lead Brandon behind the den's wards, and Brandon not wanting to leave. Finally, it seemed the two decided to fight alongside one another rather than with each other.

A bullet whizzed past Bram's ear, and he pounced on another soldier, tearing the gun from his hands.

So far, the tank had been quiet, not letting out a single shot, and Bram could only pray it was there for show and not to take them out.

A wolf could outrun a bullet if they were up to full strength and saw it ahead of time.

They couldn't live through a tank.

Right as he went to take out another soldier at Gideon's back, he fell to his knees, his ears ringing so loudly he couldn't catch his breath. A helicopter lowered itself, large speakers blaring an ultrasonic sound hanging out of its open doors. Blood seeped through Bram's fingers when he pressed his hands to his ears.

Holy hell. Every single wolf—including Gideon—was down, the wavelength too much for their sensitive ears.

Bram looked over at Charlotte and Shane, who were holding hands as they tried to pick themselves up, blood and cuts covering their bodies. Charlotte hadn't fully healed from her torture, nor had Shane from his initial change.

And Bram was too far away to help them.

He used all of his strength to at least get to Gideon's side. Maybe together he and his Alpha could somehow take down the helicopter. If they could do that, they had a chance.

He shouldn't have worried.

The Pack was made up of more than wolves, after all.

The few humans who were part of their Pack had continued fighting. In fact, they were covering the downed wolves, using weapons to take out any human soldier that got too close.

But they weren't the ones that saved them all.

Leah led the witches of their Pack as they strode powerfully toward the helicopter. Two earth witches blocked anyone from coming near them, throwing mounds of dirt up into the air to create a wall of protection.

The fire witches scorched anyone that got too close, their flames licking up toward the helicopter itself.

And Leah, soft and sweet Leah, held up her hands, bringing forth a wave of water from the neighboring lake from *behind* Montag's people. Her jaw set, she raised her hands higher, and the wave crashed down on top of the helicopter. The sound of screeching metal hitting the ground before becoming waterlogged was the best fucking sound Bram had ever heard.

He stood on shaky legs next to Gideon once the ultrasonic waves weren't hitting them anymore, his eyes wide.

"Holy fuck," Bram whispered.

"And she's ours," his Alpha said with a prideful growl.

The fighting continued, but the feeling was different, more triumphant. Ryder shot past them, running toward Leah, who looked to be swaying on her feet. That must have taken out most of her energy reserves. In fact, many of the weaker wolves on the field went to go pick up the fallen witches who had used the last of their powers to save them all. Ryder led the crew back to the den, and Bram knew he would be forever grateful for the witches and humans who had saved them all.

Bram and Gideon continued to fight as Kameron passed them, Walker on his heels. The Healer would kneel down to Heal a fallen wolf before moving on to the next, essentially performing battlefield triage. The man had to be working on a case by case basis to reserve his energy because there was no way Walker would make it any longer without doing so. Kameron stayed by Walker's side, protecting his brother and fellow triplet when he couldn't protect himself.

Brothers themselves, Max and Mitchell fought side by side, Mitchell with a determined grace that surprised Bram, and Max with a manic stride that put fear into anyone in his wake. When Mitchell took a bullet to the arm, Max jumped several feet into the air to pounce on the man who had shot his brother, ripping the gun from the man's hands before he had a chance to take a second shot.

The Talons were winning, but things weren't over.

They kept moving toward where Montag was as the man stood by his precious tank as if nothing would ever be able to touch him.

Bram would see the man dead.

Tonight.

He'd hurt *both* of his mates, and deserved all the pain that came to him.

"Now!" Montag yelled at that exact moment, and Bram hit the ground—as did each wolf around him.

The tank fired, and Bram's heart sank. They couldn't outrun this. There was no way they'd be able to, not with the firepower Montag had at his disposal.

Only the shot went over their heads...right into the wards that kept the den safe. Bram looked over his shoulder as the wards became fully visible, a kind of film coating them like a bubble trapped on the ground. Only the cracks that had formed earlier were now even larger.

Entire pieces of the wards fell away, and Bram knew this could be the end.

Only the wards didn't fall.

He narrowed his eyes right at the edge of them, shock slamming into him.

The elders of the Pack, as well as the witches who had to be exhausted, were holding up their arms, chanting and using every once of themselves as they reinforced what was left of the wards.

Ryder was physically carrying Leah as she chanted, her face deathly pale, but Brie was also there, holding up those who couldn't stand themselves.

They were Pack. They were family.

And they wouldn't fucking let Montag win.

Bram screamed, his wolf at the fore. This was why he was wolf, why he was stronger than anyone he knew other than the Alphas and Heirs.

It was for this moment.

He ran past the humans in front of him, pushing them away with his claws as he moved toward Montag. He could feel Shane and Charlotte on his heels, their mating bond pulsating like he hadn't thought possible.

They might not have the trinity bond, but their bond *was* different, and he knew exactly what to do with it.

Shane took out two soldiers on his right, Charlotte another two on his left. And Bram went straight for Montag's throat. Another bullet hit his side, but he barely felt it.

Montag screamed, trying to fight Bram off, but Bram was stronger.

Far stronger.

Bram wrapped his hand around Montag's neck, letting his claws out fully so they dug into the other man's skin.

And squeezed

When the other man fell, Bram didn't let out a sigh of relief. He didn't scream in joy and purpose that the man who had all but taken everything he could from the wolves was dead.

Bram turned his back on the body of the former General who had taken it one step too far and growled. "Give me your hands." He held out his own, and Charlotte and Bram put their palms in his without asking why.

"Now pull on your bond," Bram ordered. "That bit of energy that you feel? It's for us. For right now. Push it out and take out that fucking tank."

Charlotte's eyes widened. "Are you sure?"

"We can do that?" Shane asked.

He didn't know why he knew it, but he did, and he wasn't going to ignore the instinct thrumming through his veins.

"We can. And we will." His mates let out a collective breath, and the two of them turned toward the tank with him. He did as he'd told them, pulling on the energy that had allowed him to find Charlotte, the one that had brought him into the Talons when he had been afraid it wouldn't work.

Light shot from the sky as fire erupted from the earth. He had never heard of this before but knew this was a gift from the moon goddess herself.

A gift.

One he could never repay.

The fire engulfed the tank, and the lightning broke it into pieces. The machine that had almost taken out their entire den, their elders, their submissives, their children, *their future*, was gone.

There might be more, but for now, this was what they had been able to do.

Cheers erupted from the battlefield as the wolves shouted out their victories, the human soldiers either dead or surrendering. Montag's evil would be no more, the idea of a serum and what Shane could do for him hopefully dead along with him.

This wouldn't be the end. It couldn't be. They'd just had a major battle in the middle of a forest where people *had* to be watching. The government would come with questions, but Bram knew they would have their own answers. His people had defended themselves, and that would have to be enough.

Shane grabbed his shoulders and shook Bram from his thoughts. "You did it. You fucking did it." He kissed him hard, and Bram growled.

"*We* did it," he corrected before pulling Charlotte into a kiss. "We all did it."

"I love you," she whispered to both of them. "I...I am so fucking glad I get to say that again after what just happened." Dirt and blood covered her face, and Bram used his thumb and her tears to try to clean some of it away.

"I've never been happier to hear it," he said honestly. "Now, let's go see our people."

"Our people," Shane said softly as he looked over the field at the fallen men and women he had once fought alongside. "I...I think I need that."

Charlotte wrapped herself around Shane's middle as Bram did the same to his side. "We did it. We really did it."

"Now, let's clean up the mess," Bram added.

And they would. They would clean up not only the bodies on the ground and the burnt metal littering the forest floor, but they would also have to find a way to work through the atrocities Montag had committed.

It wasn't over.

Not by a long shot.

But for now, Bram would take this small victory. He'd hold his mates, learn his new Pack, and let his wolf come to the surface through it all.

Because he'd discovered something he'd known all along.

He was wolf.

He was Pack.

And he was *theirs*.

AVERY

Avery set her phone down and watched the battle unfold on the screen in front of her. Her mind was a half step behind the movements, but she tried to soak it all in. She couldn't comprehend it, couldn't understand how this could be happening.

The wolves and humans were fighting each other live on the screen, and yet no one was doing anything about it. From what the feed had shown, what looked like a military unit had come out of nowhere and attacked the shifters.

The wolves hadn't been doing anything but existing, and yet these people wanted them dead.

She watched as a dark-haired man tried to save another man who had just taken a bullet. They yelled at one another before beginning to fight side by side. What kind of strength did these wolves have if they could still stand for one another like that?

She was in awe.

Yet beneath it all, stark fear and shame slid through her.

She continued to watch as more wolves fell but even more humans did the same. Through it all, she kept her attention on one man, though.

The man in the uniform who stayed behind it all, not willing to get his hands dirty. It shouldn't have surprised her, and yet it did.

It devastated her.

When the older man finally began to fight, she knew this would be the end. There was no way he could win without cheating, and though he *would* cheat if he could, there wasn't enough time.

Avery watched as her father died before her eyes, but she didn't shed a tear.

She couldn't for the man who had betrayed everything inside her and even worse, betrayed the world she'd learned to love.

The news anchors commentating kept saying over and over again that Washington had nothing to do with this and the humans fighting were breaking the law—committing *treason* and *murder*.

And yet, when her father fell, his eyes glassy and empty, she felt nothing.

What had her father done?

She put her hands on the table, her body shaking.

It wasn't over, not completely. Her father would never work alone. There had to be someone else out there, something coming that the wolves might not suspect.

She looked around at her small apartment and the world she had created for herself when everything had fallen apart around her.

It seemed it had collapsed once again.

She was only a human, a daughter with no power, but somehow, *somehow*, she'd find a way to help.

It was the only thing she could do.

But Avery thought, with a sad and horrific realization, she might be too late.

Again.

EPILOGUE

A *month later*
Charlotte panted as she came down from her high, her two men on either side of her, their bodies slick with sweat and heat. She fell to the mattress, Bram behind her, Shane in front of her, the feeling of them still deep inside her making her need to come all over again.

She tried to catch her breath, but she couldn't. Instead, she just licked her lips and did her best to keep her men close.

"We need to do that again," Shane said sleepily, his voice raw. "I mean, dear God, we need to do that again."

Bram laughed behind her, his hand on her hip, his fingers brushing along Shane's. "If we do that every day, we might not have enough energy to do anything else."

"I'm okay with that," Charlotte said softly. "Let's just catch our breath and then go at it again. I think there's a position or two we haven't tried yet."

Shane pulled away slightly to looked down at her. "Really? Which ones?"

She swatted at him then winced at both men slowly pulled out of her. Bram ran a warm washcloth over each of them before coming back to spoon her from behind.

"We have patrol later today," Bram said. "All three of us are Talon lieutenants now, we can't just have sex all day and forget to protect our Alpha."

Even as Charlotte warmed at the thought of duty and purpose, she groaned. "Fine, we'll stick by Gideon's side and watch the Pack and be all amazing and strong, but when we're done, I want to try that one with my leg up in the air like we saw in that book. Okay?"

Shane kissed her hard, and she laughed. "I love the way you make plans. I wouldn't put it past you to have a sex list somewhere."

She blushed and lowered her head. She would not be telling them she'd highlighted certain parts of that book so she could come back and make a list later. There was only so much of her dorkiness she could divulge.

Bram bit her shoulder, and she moaned. "We need to shower. Separately. Or we'll be late. We're the new kids to the Pack, and I don't want to be the slackers."

She turned so she faced him, and Shane snuggled firmly into her backside. "Thanks for keeping us in line."

He smiled at her, and she fell that much more in love with him. If the man knew that every time he smiled she fell for him all over again, it would be dangerous. "I do what I have to."

They hugged as one, the three of them finding their own rhythm now. In the month since the battle that had been splashed all over the airwaves, every single shifter had been changed irrevocably. Times were uncertain, and though the human government had assured them the attack wasn't their idea, everyone was still on edge as to what would happen next.

The sanctions and laws surrounding the wolves were coming out of committee soon, and Charlotte knew that claws and fangs might not be able to fight the next wave coming at them.

But no matter what, she knew she wasn't alone. She had a new Pack, one that had taken her in just as the Redwoods had all those years before. She had her two mates, the two men who loved her and fought by her side. They didn't see her as weak. They saw her as an equal.

As they held her, she sighed into them, wanting to keep them close forever. She'd once thought the moon goddess had forsaken her, and fate had betrayed what she'd held dear. But she'd been wrong.

She'd been tested in the fiery depths of her own personal hell and had come out stronger.

She was now a Talon, a family to the Redwoods, and a wolf with two mates. A triad, a lieutenant, and a wolf with a purpose.

She was Charlotte, and she was whole.

The world had better be prepared because her Pack, *all* Packs were ready to fight back and battle for who they were.

Forever.

Coming Next in the Talon Pack World

FRACTURED SILENCE

It's time for Parker, Brandon, and newly found Avery to have their story.

A Note from Carrie Ann

Thank you so much for reading **WOLF BETRAYED**. I do hope if you liked this story, that you would please leave a review where you bought the book and on Goodreads. Not only does a review spread the word to other readers, they let us authors know if you'd like to see more stories like this from us. I love hearing from readers and talking to them when I can. If you want to make sure you know what's coming next from me, you can sign up for my newsletter at www.CarrieAnnRyan.com; follow me on twitter at @CarrieAnnRyan, or like my Facebook page. I also have a Facebook Fan Club where we have trivia, chats, and other goodies. You guys are the reason I get to do what I do and I thank you.

Make sure you're signed up for my MAILING LIST so you can know when the next releases are available as well as find giveaways and FREE READS.

The Talon Pack series is an ongoing series. I hope you get a chance to catch up! The prequel, Wicked Wolf is out now and is about Gina and Quinn. Tattered Loyalties, Talon Pack Book 1, centers around the Alpha of the Talon Pack, Gideon, and his mate, Brie. An Alpha's Choice, Talon Pack Book 2, is also out. It's about Finn and Brynn and how they found their fate. Mated in Mist, Book 3, features the Heir, Ryder, and his mate, Leah.

Next up in the series is FRACTURED SILENCE. It features, Parker, Brandon, and Leah. You'll be able to read them in 2017!

The Talon Pack (Following the Redwood Pack Series):
Book 1: Tattered Loyalties
Book 2: An Alpha's Choice
Book 3: Mated in Mist
Book 4: Wolf Betrayed
Book 5: Fractured Silence (Coming April 2017)

Want to keep up to date with the next Carrie Ann Ryan Release? Receive Text Alerts easily!
Text CARRIE to 24587

About Carrie Ann and her Books

New York Times and USA Today Bestselling Author Carrie Ann Ryan never thought she'd be a writer. Not really. No, she loved math and science and even went on to graduate school in chemistry. Yes, she read as a kid and devoured teen fiction and Harry Potter, but it wasn't until someone handed her a romance book in her late teens that she realized that there was something out there just for her. When another author suggested she use the voices in her head for good and not evil, The Redwood Pack and all her other stories were born.

Carrie Ann is a bestselling author of over twenty novels and novellas and has so much more on her mind (and on her spreadsheets *grins*) that she isn't planning on giving up her dream anytime soon.

www.CarrieAnnRyan.com

Redwood Pack Series:
Book 1: An Alpha's Path
Book 2: A Taste for a Mate
Book 3: Trinity Bound
Redwood Pack Box Set (Contains Books 1-3)
Book 3.5: A Night Away
Book 4: Enforcer's Redemption
Book 4.5: Blurred Expectations
Book 4.7: Forgiveness
Book 5: Shattered Emotions
Book 6: Hidden Destiny
Book 6.5: A Beta's Haven
Book 7: Fighting Fate
Book 7.5: Loving the Omega

Book 7.7: The Hunted Heart
Book 8: Wicked Wolf
The Complete Redwood Pack Box Set (Contains Books 1-7.7)

The Talon Pack (Following the Redwood Pack Series):
Book 1: Tattered Loyalties
Book 2: An Alpha's Choice
Book 3: Mated in Mist
Book 4: Wolf Betrayed
Book 5: Fractured Silence (Coming April 2017)

Montgomery Ink:
Book 0.5: Ink Inspired
Book 0.6: Ink Reunited
Book 1: Delicate Ink
The Montgomery Ink Box Set (Contains Books 0.5, 0.6, 1)
Book 1.5: Forever Ink
Book 2: Tempting Boundaries
Book 3: Harder than Words
Book 4: Written in Ink
Book 4.5: Hidden Ink
Book 5: Ink Enduring
Book 6: Ink Exposed (Coming November 2016)
Book 6.5: Adoring Ink (Coming January 2017)
Book 7: Inked Expressions (Coming June 2017)

The Gallagher Brothers Series:
A Montgomery Ink Spin Off Series
Book 1: Love Restored (Coming September 2016)
Book 2: Passion Restored (Coming February 2017)
Book 3: Hope Restored (Coming July 2017)

The Branded Pack Series:
(Written with Alexandra Ivy)
Book 1: Stolen and Forgiven
Book 2: Abandoned and Unseen
Book 3: Buried and Shadowed

Dante's Circle Series:
Book 1: Dust of My Wings
Book 2: Her Warriors' Three Wishes
Book 3: An Unlucky Moon
The Dante's Circle Box Set (Contains Books 1-3)
Book 3.5: His Choice
Book 4: Tangled Innocence
Book 5: Fierce Enchantment
Book 6: An Immortal's Song
Book 7: Prowled Darkness
The Complete Dante's Circle Series (Contains Books 1-7)

Holiday, Montana Series:
Book 1: Charmed Spirits
Book 2: Santa's Executive
Book 3: Finding Abigail
The Holiday, Montana Box Set (Contains Books 1-3)
Book 4: Her Lucky Love
Book 5: Dreams of Ivory
The Complete Holiday, Montana Box Set (Contains Books 1-5)

The Happy Ever After Series:
Flame and Ink

Single Title:
Finally Found You

Excerpt: Wicked Wolf

From New York Times Bestselling Author Carrie Ann Ryan's Redwood Pack Series

There were times to drool over a sexy wolf.

Sitting in the middle of a war room disguised as a board meeting was not one of those times.

Gina Jamenson did her best not to stare at the dark-haired, dark-eyed man across the room. The hint of ink peeking out from under his shirt made her want to pant. She *loved* ink and this wolf clearly had a lot of it. Her own wolf within nudged at her, a soft brush beneath her skin, but she ignored her. When her wolf whimpered, Gina promised herself that she'd go on a long run in the forest later. She didn't understand why her wolf was acting like this, but she'd deal with it when she was in a better place. She just couldn't let her wolf have control right then—even for a man such as the gorgeous specimen a mere ten feet from her.

Today was more important than the wants and feelings of a half wolf, half witch hybrid.

Today was the start of a new beginning.

At least that's what her dad had told her.

Considering her father was also the Alpha of the Redwood Pack, he would be in the know. She'd been adopted into the family when she'd been a young girl. A rogue wolf during the war had killed her parents, setting off a long line of events that had changed her life.

As it was, Gina wasn't quite sure how she'd ended up in the meeting between the two Packs, the Redwoods and the Talons. Sure, the Packs had met before over the past fifteen years of their treaty, but this meeting seemed different.

This one seemed more important somehow.

And they'd invited—more like *demanded*—Gina to attend.

At twenty-six, she knew she was the youngest wolf in the room by far. Most of the wolves were around her father's age, somewhere in the hundreds. The dark-eyed wolf might have been slightly younger than that, but only slightly if the power radiating off of him was any indication.

Wolves lived a long, long time. She'd heard stories of her people living into their thousands, but she'd never met any of the wolves who had. The oldest wolf she'd met was a friend of the family, Emeline, who was over five hundred. That number boggled her mind even though she'd grown up knowing the things that went bump in the night were real.

Actually, she *was* one of the things that went bump in the night.

"Are we ready to begin?" Gideon, the Talon Alpha, asked, his voice low. It held that dangerous edge that spoke of power and authority.

Her wolf didn't react the way most wolves would, head and eyes down, shoulders dropped. Maybe if she'd been a weaker wolf, she'd have bowed to his power, but as it was, her wolf was firmly entrenched within the Redwoods. Plus, it wasn't as if Gideon was *trying* to make her bow just then. No, those words had simply been spoken in his own voice.

Commanding without even trying.

Then again, he *was* an Alpha.

Kade, her father, looked around the room at each of his wolves and nodded. "Yes. It is time."

Their formality intrigued her. Yes, they were two Alphas who held a treaty and worked together in times of war, but she had thought they were also friends.

Maybe today was even more important than she'd realized.

Gideon released a sigh that spoke of years of angst and worries. She didn't know the history of the Talons as well as she probably should have, so she didn't know exactly why there was always an air of sadness and pain around the Alpha.

Maybe after this meeting, she'd be able to find out more.

Of course, in doing so, she'd have to *not* look at a certain wolf in the corner. His gaze was so intense she was sure he was studying her. She felt it down in her bones, like a fiery caress that promised something more.

Or maybe she was just going crazy and needed to find a wolf to scratch the itch.

She might not be looking for a mate, but she wouldn't say no to something else. Wolves were tactile creatures after all.

"Gina?"

She blinked at the sound of Kade's voice and turned to him.

She was the only one standing other than the two wolves in charge of security—her uncle Adam, the Enforcer, and the dark-eyed wolf.

Well, *that* was embarrassing.

She kept her head down and forced herself not to blush. From the heat on her neck, she was pretty sure she'd failed in the latter.

"Sorry," she mumbled then sat down next to another uncle, Jasper, the Beta of the Pack.

Although the Alphas had called this meeting, she wasn't sure what it would entail. Each Alpha had come with their Beta, a wolf in charge of security...and her father had decided to bring her.

Her being there didn't make much sense in the grand scheme of things since it put the power on the Redwoods' side, but she wasn't about to question authority in front of another Pack. That at least had been ingrained in her training.

"Let's get started then," Kade said after he gave her a nod. "Gideon? Do you want to begin?"

Gina held back a frown. They *were* acting more formal than usual, so that hadn't been her imagination. The Talons and the Redwoods had formed a treaty during the latter days of the war between the Redwoods and the Centrals. It wasn't as though these were two newly acquainted Alphas meeting for the first time. Though maybe when it came to Pack matters, Alphas couldn't truly be friends.

What a lonely way to live.

"It's been fifteen years since the end of the Central War, yet there hasn't been a single mating between the two Packs," Gideon said, shocking her.

Gina blinked. Really? That couldn't be right. She was sure there had to have been *some* cross-Pack mating.

Right?

"That means that regardless of the treaties we signed, we don't believe the moon goddess has seen fit to fully accept us as a unit," Kade put in.

"What do you mean?" she asked, then shut her mouth. She was the youngest wolf here and wasn't formally titled or ranked. She should *not* be speaking right now.

She felt the gaze of the dark-eyed wolf on her, but she didn't turn to look. Instead, she kept her head down in a show of respect to the Alphas.

"You can ask questions, Gina. It's okay," Kade said, the tone of his voice not changing, but, as his daughter, she heard the softer edge. "And what I mean is, mating comes from the moon goddess. Yes, we can find our own versions of mates by not bonding fully, but a true bond, a true potential mate, is chosen by the moon goddess. That's how it's always been in the past."

Gideon nodded. "There haven't been many matings within the Talons in general."

Gina sucked in a breath, and the Beta of the Talons, Mitchell, turned her way. "Yes," Mitchell said softly. "It's that bad. It could be that in this period of change within our own pack hierarchy, our members just haven't found mates yet, but that doesn't seem likely. There's something else going on."

Gina knew Gideon—as well as the rest of his brothers and cousins—had come into power at some point throughout the end of the Central War during a period of the Talon's own unrest, but she didn't know the full history. She wasn't even sure Kade or the rest of the Pack royalty did.

There were some things that were intensely private within a Pack that could not—and should not—be shared.

Jasper tapped his fingers along the table. As the Redwood Beta, it was his job to care for their needs and recognize hidden threats that the Enforcer and Alpha might not see. The fact that he was here told Gina that the Pack could be in trouble from something *within* the Pack, rather than an outside force that Adam, the Enforcer, would be able to see through his own bonds and power.

"Since Finn became the Heir to the Pack at such a young age, it has changed a few things on our side," Jasper said softly. Finn was her brother, Melanie and

Kade's oldest biological child. "The younger generation will be gaining their powers and bonds to the goddess earlier than would otherwise be expected." Her uncle looked at her, and she kept silent. "That means the current Pack leaders will one day not have the bonds we have to our Pack now. But like most healthy Packs, that doesn't mean we're set aside. It only means we will be there to aid the new hierarchy while they learn their powers. That's how it's always been in our Pack, and in others, but it's been a very long time since it's happened to us."

"Gina will one day be the Enforcer," Adam said from behind her. "I don't know when, but it will be soon. The other kids aren't old enough yet to tell who will take on which role, but since Gina is in her twenties, the shifts are happening."

The room grew silent, with an odd sense of change settling over her skin like an electric blanket turned on too high.

She didn't speak. She'd known about her path, had dreamed the dreams from the moon goddess herself. But that didn't mean she wanted the Talons to know all of this. It seemed...private somehow.

"What does this have to do with mating?" she asked, wanting to focus on something else.

Gideon gave her a look, and she lowered her eyes. He might not be her Alpha, but he was still a dominant wolf. Yes, she hadn't lowered her eyes before, but she'd been rocked a bit since Adam had told the others of her future. She didn't want to antagonize anyone when Gideon clearly wanted to show his power. Previously, everything had been casual; now it clearly was not.

Kade growled beside her. "Gideon."

The Talon Alpha snorted, not smiling, but moved his gaze. "It's fun to see how she reacts."

"She's my daughter and the future Enforcer."

"*She* is right here, so how about you answer my question?"

Jasper chuckled by her side, and Gina wondered how quickly she could reach the nearest window and jump. It couldn't be that far. She wouldn't die from the fall or anything, and she'd be able to run home.

Quickly.

"Mating," Kade put in, the laughter in his eyes fading, "is only a small part of the problem. When we sent Caym back to hell with the other demons, it changed the power structure within the Packs as well as outside them. The Centrals who fought against us died because they'd lost their souls to the demon. The Centrals that had hidden from the old Alphas ended up being lone wolves. They're not truly a Pack yet because the goddess hasn't made anyone an Alpha."

"Then you have the Redwoods, with a hierarchy shift within the younger generation," Gideon said. "And the Talons' new power dynamic is only fifteen years old, and we haven't had a mating in long enough that it's starting to worry us."

"Not that you'd say that to the rest of the Pack," Mitchell mumbled.

"It's best they don't know," Gideon said, the sounds of an old argument telling Gina there was more going on here than what they revealed.

Interesting.

"There aren't any matings between our two Packs, and I know the trust isn't fully there," Kade put in then sighed. "I don't know how to fix that myself. I don't think I can."

"You're the Alpha," Jasper said calmly. "If you *tell* them to get along with the other wolves, they will, and for the most part, they have. But it isn't as authentic as if they find that trust on their own. We've let them go this long on their own, but now, I think we need to find another way to have our Packs more entwined."

The dark-eyed wolf came forward then. "You've seen something," he growled.

Dear goddess. His voice.

Her wolf perked, and she shoved her down. This wasn't the time.

"We've seen...something, Quinn," Kade answered.

Quinn. That was his name.

Sexy.

And again, *so* not the time.

Tattered Loyalties

From New York Times Bestselling Author Carrie Ann Ryan's Talon Pack Series

When the great war between the Redwoods and the Centrals occurred three decades ago, the Talon Pack risked their lives for the side of good. After tragedy struck, Gideon Brentwood became the Alpha of the Talons. But the Pack's stability is threatened, and he's forced to take mate—only the one fate puts in his path is the woman he shouldn't want.

Though the daughter of the Redwood Pack's Beta, Brie Jamenson has known peace for most of her life. When she finds the man who could be her mate, she's shocked to discover Gideon is the Alpha wolf of the Talon Pack. As a submissive, her strength lies in her heart, not her claws. But if her new Pack disagrees or disapproves, the consequences could be fatal.

As the worlds Brie and Gideon have always known begin to shift, they must face their challenges together in order to help their Pack and seal their bond. But when the Pack is threatened from the inside, Gideon doesn't know who he can trust and Brie's life could be forfeit in the crossfire. It will take the strength of an Alpha and the courage of his mate to realize where true loyalties lie.

Delicate Ink

From New York Times Bestselling Author Carrie Ann Ryan's Montgomery Ink Series

On the wrong side of thirty, Austin Montgomery is ready to settle down. Unfortunately, his inked sleeves and scruffy beard isn't the suave business appearance some women crave. Only finding a woman who can deal with his job, as a tattoo artist and owner of Montgomery Ink, his seven meddling siblings, and his own gruff attitude won't be easy.

Finding a man is the last thing on Sierra Elder's mind. A recent transplant to Denver, her focus is on opening her own boutique. Wanting to cover up scars that run deeper than her flesh, she finds in Austin a man that truly gets to her—in more ways than one.

Although wary, they embark on a slow, tempestuous burn of a relationship. When blasts from both their pasts intrude on their present, however, it will take more than a promise of what could be to keep them together.

Dust of My Wings

From New York Times Bestselling Author Carrie Ann Ryan's Dante's Circle Series

Humans aren't as alone as they choose to believe. Every human possesses a trait of supernatural that lays dormant within their genetic make-up. Centuries of diluting and breeding have allowed humans to think they are alone and untouched by magic. But what happens when something changes?
Neat freak lab tech, Lily Banner lives her life as any ordinary human. She's dedicated to her work and loves to hang out with her friends at Dante's Circle, their local bar. When she discovers a strange blue dust at work she meets a handsome stranger holding secrets – and maybe her heart. But after a close call with a thunderstorm, she may not be as ordinary as she thinks.
Shade Griffin is a warrior angel sent to Earth to protect the supernaturals' secrets. One problem, he can't stop leaving dust in odd places around town. Now he has to find every ounce of his dust and keep the presence of the supernatural a secret. But after a close encounter with a sexy lab tech and a lightning quick connection, his millennia old loyalties may shift and he could lose more than just his wings in the chaos.
Warning: Contains a sexy angel with a choice to make and a green-eyed lab tech who dreams of a dark-winged stranger. Oh yeah, and a shocking spark that's sure to leave them begging for more.